"A brilliant mind altering, intergalactic delight. Brimming with humour and flair. *Greensmith* marks Aliya Whiteley's distinctive talents as something to get excited about."
Irenosen Okojie, award-winning author of *Nudibranch, Butterfly Fish* and *Speak Gigantular*

Greensmith is a head-spinning, brain-expanding journey through the universe, alternating between wildly abstract concepts and meticulously detailed character studies. Funny, resolutely British and sometimes startlingly mournful, *Greensmith* proves that Aliya Whiteley is capable of producing stunning work in any genre.
Tim Major, author of *Hope Island* and *Snakeskins*

Aliya Whiteley takes her singular voice to the cosmos in this madly imaginative, affecting and witty novel. *Greensmith*'s pages teem with life and wonder – it's the best kind of mind-bender
M.T. Hill, author of *Zero Bomb* and *The Breach*

Fans of Aliya Whiteley's work will have come to expect the unexpected and *Greensmith* delivers generously on this score. From the humble seed of botanical librarian, Patricia Greensmith, springs an exuberant adventure across time and space, busting with questions of mortality and morality, identity and biology. Told with real heart and appealingly Phythonesque humour, this is a gloriously compact tardis of a book.
Vicki Jarrett, author of *Always North*

"A radiant, sensational samba across the stars and a paean to the wonders in the overlooked and the everyday... Penelope Greensmith will capture your heart."
E.J. Swift, author of *Paris Adrift* and *The Osiris Project* trilogy

Also available from Unsung Stories

GREENSMITH

ALIYA WHITELEY

UNSUNG
STORIES

Published by Unsung Stories

3 Rosslyn Road, London E17 9EU,
United Kingdom

www.unsungstories.co.uk

First edition published in 2020
First impression

Paperback ISBN: 978-1-912658-07-7
ePub ISBN: 978-1-912658-08-4

Edited by George Sandison
Proofreading by Dan Coxon

Cover Artwork © Sam Chivers 2020

Cover design by Vince Haig
Text design by Cox Design Limited
Typesetting by George Sandison

Printed in the UK by Clays Ltd, Elcograf S.p.A.

For B.J.C.W,
who proves that change is inevitable,
and for Iris.

"I have never attempted to achieve my potential. What could be worse than to achieve one's potential so early in life? I leave it, on the horizon, glimmering..."

Peter Cook, November 1994, during his last television interview.

CAPTURE **ONE**

I'm alone, as usual.

It's hot in my new kitchen. I lit the range cooker a few days ago, even though the sun is still shining on and down with the urgent exhaustion of late summer. I'm already picturing making pies and stews, and digging out my winter clothes.

Will I ever escape the woman I've become? Can we break free from ourselves by thought alone?

Of course not. That's why this situation requires online dating.

The screen says *Describe Yourself and Your Ideal Partner* and all I've got so far is:

Hi! My name is Penelope Greensmith and I'm a 52-year-old divorcee with one daughter (grown up). I'm a bio-librarian and I've been working very hard on a project since before she was born, but recently I realised that I will never complete it, no matter how hard I work. That's not a terrible thing to know in itself, and I will endeavour to continue onwards. But it has made me realise that I need to be bigger than this one project.

I need to be part of the world.

So, I'm looking for excitement and enthusiasm in a partner. I'm looking for someone who can bring out aspects of me that I never knew existed. I don't care for good looks or money or any of the usual daydreams. I just want you to find me as interesting as I find you.

*I suspect that being interesting is a concept that other people apply to a personality rather than a concept that one gets to apply to one's self. Let me explain. When I label a floral specimen to apply the appropriate metadata tags for storage purposes, I put down a number of terms, including colour, texture, segmentation, and geographical information. Then I add a personal tag – just one word – simply to remind me of what it made me feel when I examined that bloom, worshipped it, and lavished it with the kind of attention I now wish to have lavished upon me. I have used words such as **fragrant** and **exquisite**. I never repeat a word, so it is in fact a useless classification tool for anything other than my own selfish need to remember it.*

*I've never applied the tag of **interesting** to a flower, but one day I might. **Interesting** is a quality that doesn't grow from within, and the use of it would say more about me than about the flower to which I apply it. Some terms define the scientist, and not the specimen at all.*

So be my scientist, and make me into your exquisite, fragrant specimen, and I will do the same for you.

Look at that.

I ended up being myself again. No matter where I go, there I am.

Hello. My name is Penelope Greensmith. I don't want to know anything about you and I hope you'll want to know even less about me. Let's discover each other together.

Somewhere between these attempts at finding love/sex/something indescribable lies a version of myself I can live with.

I'm Penny, and you're anybody. You're up for anything. Except pain and public embarrassment.

I want to put that my ideal partner would not have fought in, or even condoned, the War – but that rules out so many people. Plus, should I really demand a fellow pacifist as a soulmate so aggressively?

I must stand firm on this point. I have never wanted that war in my life.

Now it's over – is it really over? – it isn't what I thought it was. Whether it's being fought or not – in the ground, in the air, in the electrically charged spaces between – it has changed everything. It is still changing me.

DURING **THE WAR**

For a long time Penelope Greensmith thought the War would end without reaching its roots deep enough into the world to disturb her project.

But the War did not find any end.

It grew.

It stretched itself as far as the nearby town, but it did not arrive through the roots at all. There was no trembling sensation in the suffering soil. Instead it appeared in the air. Not visibly, at first. The computers transmitted it, as a call to arms. It jumped to radio, with hosts using active words, dangerous words. Then flags appeared, flapping from first-floor windows. *Our country's history is under attack!* Conversations floated to her ears as she sipped tea in the cafe of the garden centre. Those were followed by leaflets through her letterbox, tangling together concepts of attack and defence, necessity and patriotism.

Before the War could touch Penelope, she fled. She used her life savings to buy a cottage on top of a small hill, in the countryside, between a couple of not very picturesque villages that were barely big enough to be marked on a map. She hoped nobody would ever visit them, or find her.

The removal company she employed consisted of three men. One was older, with a lined, kind face, and he was obviously in charge of the two younger men who looked around the boxes with the squint of opportunity in their eyes.

"Twenty-six boxes, fourteen marked delicate," read the older one from his tablet.

"Yes. I packed them myself. I only need you for the heavy lifting, please."

"You've got good timing," he said. "Another couple of weeks and these two are off. Signed up to do their duty. Six months in a data centre. I don't know what I'll do then. Manage on my own, I suppose." The way he said it made her think they were his sons.

The sons looked at her over the boxes, expectantly, as if she was meant to congratulate them.

"Very good," she said, in the end.

"So it says on the packing form you're a bank?" said the very thin son, who had a pencil moustache over a twitchy top lip.

"I'm not a bank. I have a bank. A flower bank."

"A flower bank," he repeated.

She didn't bother to try and explain it. She'd learned a long time ago that attempting to communicate the importance of the Collection was futile. "You need to take extra care with the boxes in this room and the study upstairs."

"We can't guarantee we'll get flowers there in one piece. Alive," said the one in charge. "We'll do our best, of course, but—"

"They're not alive," Penelope said. "It'll be fine." The removals went smoothly, and at the end of the day, once they had unpacked her boxes from their unwieldy van into the small dusty space of the cottage, she wished the sons luck.

The cottage was so very quiet, surrounded by orderly gardens whilst affording a view over miles of land below her, and yet Penelope knew better than to trust the serenity it gifted to her. She felt an uneasiness about its sturdy stone walls, as if something was coming that would penetrate them and make any faith she placed in them look foolish.

She had hoped moving house would help her feel better, but she knew the War was all around her. She thought of those two young men, and wondered what had persuaded them to sign up. They had fallen prey to an insidious, crawling mass delusion that had been carried by flags and leaflets and radio waves to their doors. Or perhaps they were just bored, and hadn't thought carefully enough about themselves, or their father.

More and more people were forgetting what normality should have been – that middle line of contentment and community, where people felt a great certainty about the happenings they collectively agreed upon. But each realisation of another event that had disappeared from historical records online, such as the Exxon Valdez Oil Spill (surely she hadn't made that up?), was a giant hand swatting at that middle line until there would come a day when there was no sign of a line at all, and everybody accepted uncertainty as the basis for their existence.

Penelope stopped looking at the internet for anything other than ordering her flowers. She shut out all variations of news, and that seemed to help. Time passed for a while in a languid stream.

She worked on. Seeds arrived from all over the world.

After a while she remembered that other things still existed, things that could not be disproven simply by being erased from a screen, so she wrote to her daughter. Lily wrote back with the surprising news that she would come and visit as soon as it was convenient. The visit, it turned out, was to announce her engagement to Kieran Something.

"So he's a teacher as well?" Penelope asked her. They sat in the herb garden together, around the circular chrome table that was incongruous amidst the rockery. It was not exactly home yet, perhaps because she couldn't afford the kind of furniture that would suit the place. She did like the range cooker that had come with it, though. That, at least, belonged there.

"An educational co-ordinator," said Lily. "He works in the same school as me. You'll like him. He would have come today but I wanted to talk to you on your own. It's been a long time. It's nobody's fault."

"No, of course," Penelope said. "Busy, busy. Both of us."

She'd made a large jug of mint tea, using leaves picked from the rockery, perfect for a summer's day, and the two of them were getting through it at speed. Drinking was often easier than talking, Penelope had noticed. She poured some more as Lily said, "About Grandad's Collection." She had never once verbally admitted the transfer of ownership from Penelope's father to Penelope herself.

"I know moving so far from anywhere seems excessive—"

Lily held up a hand. "I just want to understand."

"Why? Does that matter? I thought you didn't care for plants."

"I don't understand how it works," said her daughter, and Penelope was reminded of a serious little girl in orange dungarees who needed to know all about photosynthesis and then dismissed it as funny. But it was a funny business; life was a funny business, and that vision of the past encapsulated a revelation. Penelope remembered that people weren't bad or stupid simply because they didn't care for the same things that she cared for. They could have no memory of the Exxon Valdez disaster and yet could still be decent human beings.

Love for people, for the idea of them, sneaked back inside her and set up shop. She wanted people again. People, not plants.

"There's no way to really understand it," she told Lily. "I don't even understand it. I'm just trying to catalogue it. You don't ever have to have anything to do with it, but that doesn't change how proud I am of you anyway. You, out in the world, trying to go on with life. Getting engaged, making plans, through this awful war."

"Mum, the War is over."

"No it isn't," Penelope said, astonished.

"It's over. There's an online ceasefire. It's holding. It came into effect about a month ago."

It was too much to take in. "But the air. The plants." How to explain that she had felt the conflict, the erasing of human history, as an invisible force, through the soil, in the fall of the rain? "The environment," she said, eventually.

"The big companies backed down. Admitted they'd been covering up their own mistakes. The latest scientific reports think the Earth will recover. Have you heard about the purifying units? The ocean recyclers? It's all bouncing back. Nature does that. That's why I wondered if maybe it was time to talk to somebody about the Collection. Finally reveal it to the world. Perhaps there's a chance to reintroduce some lost varieties. Isn't that what it's for?"

Was that what it was for?

"Imagine," said Lily. "A world filled with flowers once more. A world filled with so many things that were thought lost."

"I'll think about it," she said. "How's your dad?"

"He's good. Bearing up. The new girlfriend left him."

"That was quick. How long was it, this time?"

"Four months, he said, last time I talked to him. He said that was quite a stretch, for him."

They had a conversation about the ex-husband and his love life while Penelope felt impatient at her own small, controllable limits and boundaries. As she said goodbye to Lily, with the assurance that she would look up the War on reputable sites on her laptop, she wished that she was no longer the kind of person who had a pot plant of a life. She wanted to grow outwards, and go wherever her twirling tendrils might take her.

Maybe this was her moment. The moment to share her Collection.

She tried out those feelings that evening. She took a bath and imagined getting dressed in some flimsy outfit and dancing around, maybe writing a long passionate letter to the ex-husband just to make herself feel young again.

But she was not vindictive, and could not go so far as to manufacture that emotion even when attempting to reinvent herself. So instead she poured herself a small glass of white wine and browsed the War on the laptop.

It really was over.

It was too strange to celebrate. It had become part of her hatred of humanity, and she no longer had an excuse for that hatred. She had to find a way to be better than that.

So she found a dating website affiliated to the classical music radio station she liked and started to fill it out, until she heard a noise outside the back door, in the blousy explosion of the rose garden, and realised it could only be the sound of a man coughing.

〉•〈

Penelope crouched by the sink and peeked out of the window. It was one of those clear evenings when the light had an unmatchable clarity; the stranger was thrown into bright relief against it, fine hairs standing up from the crown of his head, his eyes narrowed in concentration as he examined the exposed heart of a musk hybrid rose that she recognised as the variety Fimbriata. It had been attracting bees en masse all summer and for a moment Penelope had the thought that it had called to this man in the same way, with the promise of its sweetness.

She stood up, opened the window, and called out, "Can I help you?"

"Greetings!" he said, without looking at her. "I just had to sniff it."

"Fimbriata? They are beautiful," she agreed, but felt compelled to mention, "they are quite common. You could find them in lots of places. Including public parks and gardens."

"Quite common," he said, and laughed. It was a whole-hearted, full-bodied laugh that did not belong to the conversation.

Penelope appraised him. He was tall and slim, dressed in a pinstripe shirt with the collar loose and the sleeves rolled, and trousers that sat low on his waist. His shoes were bright green lace-ups.

"Has your car broken down?" she asked.

"No, no. I don't do cars. Would you care to join me out here?" He swept out an arm, encompassing the garden and the land beyond, and Penelope saw it afresh, how perfect it was. The War had nearly sucked away her ability to see it.

"No thanks," she said.

"Really? All right then. Do you think we could possibly talk about your Collection?"

"You want to talk about the Collection."

"If it's not too much trouble. And it would be pleasant to have the conversation out here."

He was a fellow lover of nature, and he had come to talk about her Collection, which he somehow knew about. He had sought her out. It was – what was the word she wanted?

It was mysterious.

She closed the window and walked out of the back door. The air was still warm, and the scent of the roses strong in the last remaining rays of the day. Maybe it was the glass of wine that made the moment feel separate, encapsulated, from all she had experienced before. She could feel the hairs on her forearms rising to the challenge as she stood beside him.

"Who told you about the Collection?" she asked. "Was it my daughter?"

"I sniffed it out."

"It's a bit unorthodox, actually, just turning up in people's gardens."

"It's the only place I ever do turn up. I'm trying to visit all the great formal gardens I can find. The ones with real planning and forethought. When its done well you can really get a feel what life is all about."

It was a strange way of describing his attraction to the subject, but she thought she could understand it. "Have you visited many?"

He nodded.

"I wouldn't have thought this little garden would qualify. I'm not even taking good care of it, if I'm honest."

"This garden? It is charming, but I was talking about the Collection. I'd love to see it, if you'd let me."

"The Collection isn't a garden."

He smiled at her, revealing idiosyncratic teeth. "The flowers of the planet, in the process of being catalogued and classified – that sounds like a very formal garden, wouldn't you say?"

"Who did you say told you about it?"

"Let's start again," he said. "I'm a horticulturalist. You're…"

"Penelope Greensmith."

"Yes, sorry, I'm not good with names."

"So much so you've forgotten your own?" she asked.

"You can call me Hort, if it helps. Hort for short. Could I see it?"

His eagerness reached into her, tugged at her throat. How many people had ever asked, and meant it? How many risks had she ever taken?

With the War over, in the resolution of a possible future, was it the right moment to start?

She swallowed, and said, "I suppose you could."

> • <

Sometimes it's not about what you are, but the possibility of what you might be.

That was what Penelope saw whenever she looked at the bank. It represented a future that she liked and wanted to work towards. It also represented the possibility that her past (and her father's past before her) had not been a total waste of time, which was a powerful incentive to cherish it.

She was aware of this pressure whenever she walked down the stairs to the basement.

The basement had once been a wine cellar, but the long storage racks with their semi-circular indentations were a perfect match for the metal discs that comprised the Collection. She had been working on establishing a new cataloguing system since moving in, but had yet to hit upon a solution that really appealed to her. There was the added problem that some of the discs still held dabs of paint from her father's original records, confusing the whole business.

In the yellow glow from the tulip-shaped wall lamps, Hort walked between the sets of shelves, one finger tracing along the lip of the dark wood.

"Amazing," he said. "How many are there?"

"117,000," she said. "Possibly a quarter of all flowers in the world. I get samples delivered every day, from so many places. I inherited money from my father, who married into wealth. The Collection became my father's only passion, and I inherited it. Of course, nobody really ever took it seriously, back then, before conservation really existed as an idea. We thought the planet was endlessly plentiful, didn't we?"

"They didn't believe in him?"

"The best people don't get believed in. Francis Greensmith was just one of them," she said.

He turned, and pointed a dusty finger at her. "Right. What section am I in?"

"Dianthus. Carnations."

"Each disc represents one species of carnation?"

"It's not a representation, exactly. It's a compression. Each disc contains all the information you would need to recreate that type of flower. I have a piece of equipment that presses the flower, and transfers the data."

"How does it do that?"

"I hope you'll understand that I really can't say." She walked him through the aisles and he asked all the right questions of her. They reached the lilies, and she selected her favourite from the rack. "The Easter lily. *Lilium longiflorum.* I named my daughter after it; she was born at Easter time." She pressed the small button on top of the disc that released a small 3D projection of the white trumpet-shaped bloom along with its fragrance, which hung sweetly in the musty basement for a moment before vanishing.

"Incredible," breathed Hort.

"Here," she said, on an impulse. "Hold it."

He cradled the disc. How fragile it looked in his hands.

"I wish I understood it all better," she admitted, then felt a profound embarrassment for sharing such personal information with a stranger. And he was a stranger; she tried to keep that in mind, no matter how much she wanted to confide in him. "Okay, look," she started, determined to take control of the situation, but then couldn't think of what else to say. She felt English, and constrained by her own good manners. It occurred to her that Hort wasn't English in the same way. He was certainly polite, and had the right kind of voice and attitude for a forgetful lecturer or some sort of educational professional, but something in his speech – the way he stood close to her, and the colour of those shoes – gave him away. Where was he from?

"Perhaps we should get some answers," he said. He put the disc back in precisely the right place.

"Answers?"

"To your father's techniques. I don't mean to overstep the mark, but I've been researching something similar for ages and I think it would be of great benefit to us both if we pooled our knowledge."

"Really?" It was on the tip of her tongue to reject the offer, and then she remembered the dating form on the computer and the vision of prancing round in a silky nightdress and said, "I start work at nine every morning. If you can come back then, I'll show you how I make the compressions."

"You have a machine for that, I'm guessing?"

"I call it the Vice." It was not large, and stood in plain sight in the basement, on the long oak table where she worked. A bulbous, heavy cube – she had always assumed the metal to be iron – with a small slot in its top, and a circular outlet below from which it spat the completed compressions, it bore no maker's marks. She had given up wondering about where it came from years ago.

"Magnificent! I'd love to see that."

"Perhaps," she said. She took care not to let her eyes flicker to it. It was the most personal part of her legacy.

She led the way up the stairs to the front door, and opening it revealed how time had moved fast in the basement – almost as fast as events. Night had fallen and the world looked different again. She stepped out, wrapping her cardigan over her chest, and the perimeter lights clicked on, so bright, turning the driveway into a dramatic, heightened space.

Hort followed her out and looked around the bushes and shrubs that lined the path with his apparent unfailing interest. "I love these," he said, pointing to a fuchsia bush.

She nodded. "See you in the morning, then?"

"Yes! Absolutely."

"Right. Do you know where you're going?"

"Yes."

"Okay."

"Yes."

"Goodnight, then."

Penelope stepped back into the house and closed the door. She wouldn't admit him in the morning, she decided, while her hand was still on the handle. She would make some excuse. It was all too strange for her, too far from her comfort zone.

But right now - what? Finishing the dating form? The business of it seemed unlikely to attract anybody she would want to spend time with. At its best, it might bring her someone who wanted sex, she supposed. And sex was not enough. It was not all that she was after.

She wanted that horribly aging word of companionship.

Her ex-husband's voice sneaked into her head. She hadn't heard it in years, or perhaps she had simply grown used to ignoring it. *Normal people don't turn up unannounced in your back garden*, Graham said to her, and she threw it away, threw it all: the voice, the precautions, the doubts seeded by the war that was no longer a war, the very concept of normality.

Penelope opened the front door.

Hort was standing in the same spot. "I'll wait here," he said. "Until nine in the morning." He said the time as if it was an unfamiliar notion, taking care over the words.

"What?"

"If you don't mind."

"Don't be ridiculous. Come inside. I'll show you the Vice now," she said, and ushered him inside.

"Now!' he said. "I like now."

CAPTURE **TWO**

Diversity in nature is essential, and yet it is the exact opposite of what mankind has aimed to achieve. Homogeneity rules, from the few types of crop we plant with soil-destroying regularity to the cattle we cultivate. In ourselves, too, we aim to be the same, capping it all with the narrow notion and unspendable currency of beauty.

I am not beautiful. I'm on the cusp of withering, my ovaries spent, and I am grateful that I do not have the coinage of good looks to lose. How I would have invested in the concept of it, if I had ever possessed it. Instead I ignored my large chin and have not favoured a single-minded approach to anything in my life. Such things shape us.

But I did have an unwavering methodology about my work; if I have not faltered since I inherited the Collection it is because I found no like mind to suggest a better course. No, not even when I worked for my degree in botany at a university amidst the students who should have offered freshness, or my Masters in Librarianship. Not one of them offered me a better way of life, and I didn't tell anyone about my own.

So how come I've told Hort all about it in five days?

Five days. That's all the time I have passed in his company, and every moment has taught me to no longer assume that everybody is the same on some level. People can understand me and surprise me. Well, Hort can. His mind works in such interesting ways. I start a sentence and he finishes it, but what he adds to it makes it better, more meaningful, than anything I might have said. And yet it is precisely what I wanted to say in the first place.

I can't explain how the Vice works, and neither can he. But when we stand beside it, together, it feels less implausible to say we might find an explanation one day.

He chooses muesli for breakfast this morning. Yesterday he chose toast, and the day before he opted for scrambled egg. How can that be important? And yet it is. Breakfast choices are now important to me. I watch him eat with such gusto, and I look forward to the day ahead, as we edge a little closer to getting our mutual answers.

When we find them, will he leave? How can he, if he feels it too? Surely he feels this too?

REDUCTION

"It shrinks without sacrificing information," Hort mused over the kitchen table, waving his spoon at her before thrusting it back into the bowl of muesli.

"Would compression be a better description?" said Penelope.

"Shrinkage, compression… What did your father call it?"

"He called it reduction. But that's because he said it always reminded him of jam-making."

"I beg your pardon?"

Hort's bemused expression made her laugh. "I know. He travelled the world, he learned so much, he somehow came up with this amazing, inexplicable machine. And then he described it as being similar to the process of making jam, because he used to watch my mother do just that, and he said he was always fascinated by it."

"And how does a person make jam?"

She explained the fruit, the sugar, the boiling, the sterilising, and the wrinkle test to him. "You put a spoonful on a cold plate, leave it for a minute, and then push it with your finger. If it wrinkles, it's ready."

"I don't think this line of thought is helping much," he said. "Did your mother manipulate it in some way? Were special words involved?"

She laughed. "I don't know. I don't remember her jamming process; she died just after I was born. She was German, in fact. All the money came from her side of the family, but they didn't want anything to do with my father after she died. I think they blamed him, somehow."

"Leaving you and your father alone." Hort reached across the table and squeezed her hand. She returned the pressure. Talking was coming more easily to her, and the more she did it, the more she found to say.

"I had a brother," she said. "Leonard. I never met him. He died before I was born. I think maybe that's why— That's why I've always felt quite... lonely."

He didn't reply. His thumb stroked the back of her hand, and that was all the comfort he could have given her. It was so odd, how the smallest of gestures could be so meaningful.

"Anyway..." she said, eventually.

"Yes!" Hort dropped her hand and returned to his muesli. "Compression. Reduction. What's the difference?"

Penelope drank her tea. The kitchen was bright and warm; her favourite room in the cottage first thing in the morning. "No. You're right. It's only semantics, really. Although I wonder – if you can't describe it accurately, can you ever claim to—"

"Understand it, yes, understanding things, but that's so overrated, for me, Pea. Knowing it is better than understanding it. It's the difference between standing inside a place and looking through a window at it."

She shook her head. "Still just semantics."

"You think that language choice is just the same as swimming in a different part of the same sea?" He punctuated his thoughts by waving his spoon in the air. "All higher thought relies upon the act of communication. You can't share it, you don't know it."

"So if Einstein didn't speak or write a word for twenty years he wouldn't have been a genius?"

"A creature that does not express itself is not engaged in the act of refining itself. It's the act of translation that makes thought blossom from unformed possibility to knowledge. This is delicious," he said. "What is it?"

"Muesli."

"I like muesli best, I think. But to you, it's all just breakfast, right? A question of semantics."

"And to you, every breakfast is a unique and special moment that should be not classified in one great lump of experience," she said, smiling.

He swallowed his last mouthful and said, "Touché. But we're off topic. You're certain your father left no notes about the Vice?"

"Nothing. I sorted through his papers again recently, what with the house move."

"And there are no marks on it, no signs of construction," he mused.

"I always remember him having it. But it's possible he didn't build it." She mentally reviewed the process. The flower itself was fed through the main slot. The Vice then created a disc inside itself that, once filled with the flower's information, popped out from its underbelly. There was no obvious power source, and yet it created a record, of a kind. Each disc rattled, when shaken. The seeds inside it, she had thought. But how did it create the image? She had never been brave enough to try to open it up, although gentle explorations had revealed there was no apparent way to open it, anyway.

"Have you ever…" said Hort. "I mean, have you experienced the urge to…"

"What?"

"Never mind. We're no closer, are we? I thought if I saw your process it would throw some light on it all."

"For your own research, you mean?"

He nodded.

"You've got a machine that's similar to the Vice?"

"Oh no. I suspect the Vice is unique."

"Then what's your point of reference?" she asked him.

He looked away, his face intent with concentration – was he considering the question? "Ah," he said. "Time has passed. That flew by. You made it so easy to get lost in this space. Thank you for that. It's probably time you spoke to your daughter. She'll have something to tell you about the news."

"What news?"

"Bad news."

> • <

Lily didn't pick up the call.

Hort had wandered off to the rose garden, claiming she would need time alone for some reason, so Penelope switched on the laptop and did something she hadn't done in weeks. She browsed the news outlets.

There was a rare consensus between the multicoloured harbingers of doom. A mysterious disease was sweeping across all forms of plant life on the planet. Anything that used photosynthesis to create the nutrients it needed was dying, and scientists had come together across the world to search for a cure.

The sites didn't agree on much beyond that. One claimed that genetically modified crops were responsible. Another talked of a team of British professors who had already developed a "plant vaccine" and were testing it on carrots. A third described in purple prose how people in some countries were eating their children. Articles focusing on the UK contained pictures of empty supermarket shelves and people in baseball caps with scarves over their faces carrying off large televisions. *Why is it always televisions that got looted?* she wondered. It didn't seem sensible. She took those reports with a pinch of salt.

But the video footage of the great rainforests of the Earth melting, oozing into a thick green paste, creating vast swamps – she couldn't stop watching them, so many of them, and although she would have liked to have dismissed them as doctored they were simply too amateur to remind her of the feature films she had seen about end-of-the-world scenarios. The people filming observed quietly, spoke in hushed tones, said banal things like *Look at that* or *There goes another.* Shouldn't people have been screaming? In the trial runs for the end of the world found in fiction, from Armageddon to zombies, there had been screaming and everyone had known it was the end. Yet, in this reality, nobody online was admitting any such thing.

Penelope tried to ring her daughter again, and there was still no response. She left a standard sort of message, felt the ridiculousness of it, and decided to try her ex-husband instead. He picked up straight away.

"Pen, she's with me, here," Graham said, without preamble, and that recognisable and pragmatic tone was a vast relief. "She's sleeping now. Kieran got into a fight at a supermarket over a packet of tomatoes. He was killed, she says. It's all going to hell out there."

Who was Kieran? The fiancé, she remembered, and her gratitude that he had been killed instead of Lily was strong, and instant. How quickly everybody could be divided into people that mattered and people that didn't. "But you've got her? She's safe?"

"Listen, she says you're living in the middle of nowhere."

"I'm fine."

"No, has it reached you? The virus?" Graham's voice was raw; she wondered if he had been shouting at people. He tended to do that in bad situations, but if he could make those situations better, he did.

"No, no, there's nothing, I just turned on the news and—"

"Can we come to you? It's no good here. I've got enough petrol left in the car. We can get organised once I'm there. Supplies. Defence."

"Of course," she said. "Of course."

"We'll be leaving within the hour."

He ended the call.

It was too new a disaster to be paralysed by it, even if Graham had just made it real to her, far more real than the news could ever have managed. It only seemed sensible to go out to the rose garden and tell Hort they were expecting company.

Hort, hands in pockets, head thrown back, breathing deeply, looked different. He looked older.

"It's here already," he said. "So sad." His gaze was on the Fimbriata; the tips of the leaves were turning a vivid, unpleasant shade of green and the petals looked fatter, fleshier.

"My daughter is on her way, with my ex-husband and his wife. He thinks they'll be safer. But they won't, will they?"

"No, I'm afraid not."

"Who are you?"

"I'm not from around here."

"No."

"I'm difficult to describe, which is ironic, considering."

"All the plants are dying."

"It's a kind of virus. That's not exactly right either. It's…" He shrugged. "It's very difficult to get to the point in your language, isn't it?"

"English isn't your first language?" Of course it wasn't. He spoke it perfectly, and yet each word seemed to mean something else as it emerged from him. His mouth never quite looked at home with the sentences it produced.

"Earth isn't my first language."

"Don't be flippant," she told him. "We need to do something, we need to prepare, perhaps even get to work on a cure, is that crazy? But why not us, I mean, solutions come from the strangest places."

He stood still, regarding the rose. Then he said, "Pea, you can't save it if you stay here. I've seen it before. There is nothing we can do while we're here."

"Here, in this cottage?"

"On this planet."

"What?"

"But I can take you with me. When I leave. Which is now." She stared at him. All the things he had been saying began to percolate through her brain. "We can find a cure for it together. The Vice is the key. I'm sure of it. I've been searching for something like it for so long, across the universe."

"You're saying you're a spaceman. No, that's not the word. An alien. A space alien. What do you call yourself?"

"I call myself the Horticulturalist, Pea. And I'm here to help. I promise you. I can help your planet. But not while I'm here, and it's dying around me. And it is dying." He opened his arms to her and she walked into the comfort he offered. He smelled of coffee and toast, which was odd considering he'd had muesli. "First the plants die, then the mammals, then the insects," he said. "Did you speak to Lily?"

"She was sleeping."

"That's a shame. It was realistically your last chance for a good long while. Okay, here's the thing. I'm leaving right now, and I want you to come with me. Because nobody knows that Vice like you do. And because we make a great team." He released her, and took a step back to squint up at the sun. "I have a method for travelling with a companion. For keeping a personality as intact as possible while moving through the universe, at speed, vast distances. It's a compression of self— Damn this language!" He stamped around the rose garden. "Damn it bugger it fuck it, it's knobtanglingly difficult at times, isn't it? It's quite therapeutic for swearing in, though. You knew this was coming, Pea? Didn't you?"

Penelope thought back to the feeling through the soil, in the roots, that she had long been attributing to the War. Now it had a shape, and it was not a human catastrophe at all. Unless.

"Did people make this virus? Scientists, in a lab, that kind of thing?" she asked.

Hort smiled, and shook his head. "No. Not people. People aren't the be all and end all, you know. You're not responsible for everything. You'll understand that if you come with me. You'll have a better grasp of what it means to be human, because you won't be one any more. You'll be…" He clicked his fingers until the words came. "It's like your father said. If you're the fruit now, you'll become jam."

"Reduced," said Penelope. "Squashed."

"Intensified. And we're back to semantics. We'll take the Vice, get some answers. I'll take along the Collection, too. Keep it safe. I have the perfect place for it."

"This is bizarre," she said.

The sun was shining, the sky was blue and held perfect puffed dots of cloud, and she could hear a light rain falling in the woods. No, not rain. Not rain, after all. The branches were becoming bare, and the dripping was the sound of leaves turning to liquid and falling, in soft rhythm, to the ground. Penelope listened as she examined the Fimbriata; the petals were so soft and full, and trembling. She blew on one, and it heaved, broke its form, and splashed apart.

"It's a corruption," said Hort, which made no sense to her.

"I told them to come here. Lily. Graham."

"Could you leave a key under the mat? Or just leave the door unlocked."

It had been so difficult to believe in anything for years, apart from the flowers. There had been such fighting to control the world, and what people thought of it. Could she choose, at this moment, not to believe in Hort and the virus, of the evidence of her own eyes? It would have been easy to ignore it, go back inside the cottage, for a few minutes more, at least.

But that feeling, the feeling of something coming for her. It was here. It was time to make the decision to be a different person.

"I'll be the same in some ways, right? If you reduce me."

"Every aspect of you will be recorded in incredibly accurate detail. It's a little like the Collection. Those are still flowers, really, aren't they? Down in the basement."

"In a way."

"So you'll be you. In a way."

"How does it work?"

"I take a few – hmmmm..." Hort mused over the words, while all around them the natural world dissolved, "snapshots of you, and then you won't even feel a thing."

"That doesn't tell me much."

"I know. I'm sorry. I was attempting to be reassuring rather than accurate."

"And then what?"

"We go travelling, we get our answers, and we save the universe. Maybe even Earth, too, if we're quick enough."

She remembered what he had told her three days ago, upon his arrival. "You've been looking for a cure in the formal gardens."

"Of the universe, yes. This is a universal virus."

Other places, wiped clean of flora. Other planets.

"We could wait," she said. "We could take my daughter, too."

Hort squeezed her hand between his, and said, "No. If you're coming, you're coming now. Besides, you won't exactly feel... The emotional intensity of that connection in the same way, in your new form."

"I'll forget her?"

"You'll still care. Eventually, you won't care as much."

It was that idea that helped her to make up her mind. There were only two options open to her: stay put, and protect Lily to the end; or leave, try to save the world – the universe, even, okay, why not? – and find a way to not blame herself for leaving Lily behind. To hear not caring so much could be part of the deal. Yes, that would be possible. That could work. She could function, that way.

"Okay," she said. "What happens first?"

"It's already happened. I've taken two pictures, captures, of your personality. Just moments of thought really. It gives me all the information I need. It's an internal process for me. You haven't noticed a thing. So we're all ready to go. Just say the word."

"You took these captures without my permission?"

"I wouldn't have used them if you said no," he said. "Trust me. There's no fun in travelling with a permanently pissed-off companion. If you're coming along, it's because you want to. Because we have a job to do."

"A virus to stop," she whispered. But not on Earth, and not only for Earth.

The tree branches had melted to sludge and the trunks were starting to follow suit. The roses, all of them, were fat formless blobs in a child's painting and the smell in the air, growing stronger by the second, reminded her of petrol.

She shut her eyes tight. "Don't forget to bring the Collection."

"I won't."

"Or the Vice."

"Absolutely."

"I'm trusting you," she said, with a hint of warning, and was reminded of a little girl in a blue dress standing next to a hot tray of chocolate biscuits, fresh from the oven, with her hands clasped behind her back, promising not to touch. Lily, oh Lily, Lilium longiflorum, her Easter gift, such a generous gift considering she spent her own life so meanly, parcelled out, sorted, filed away and now about to be squashed. Squashed flat.

Compression, reduction, intensification.

GREENHOUSE

I haven't felt so light in years.

So many aches and pains became standard issue as I aged. They were an unremarkable yet cumbersome kit that I strapped to myself every day as soon as I awoke. But these first seconds after being reduced – these moments are free of the tight muscles, the sore neck, the permanent niggle of the lower back. These were not serious complaints; they were simply baggage. The baggage of life.

I'm not alive any more.

The aches weren't just physical in nature. Worries also made up the weight: responsibilities, duties, a list of things that must be done each day before lying down in bed once more. I didn't realise that these were part of being human too, somehow a by-product of my own flesh, of my age, of all the experiences that had soaked into my skin.

Now I'm free of them all. How heavy they were. I revel in the sensation of being younger, and unaware of joints and bones and time.

"You okay, Pea?" says Hort. We are in the dark together. His voice is close to my right ear. I feel his touch, gentle, upon my arm.

"Good, actually."

"Great. Do you think you could…"

"What?"

"Open your eyes, then?"

"Oh. Right." How ridiculous of me. We're not in the dark at all. Well, we are. We are floating in a dark space. Perhaps in outer space.

I wait for my eyes to adjust, and feel only calmness until a new awareness tells me that something big is behind me. Something huge. A giant presence upon which I should look, but I don't want to. To look upon it will change everything, and that terrifies me. It will take all the thoughts I've ever had and put them into a tiny, true perspective.

"Turn around," says Hort. "It's okay." His hands are on my back; he twists me around and upside down, and I realise I'm in a foetal position, curled up tight. But as the Earth swims into view and fills my field of vision I spread my limbs wide, unfolding, opening to its stupendous, magnificent majesty. The blue and the green, the colours so vivid, the shining hulk of it, the living ball of it, the thriving encapsulation of creation. The presence.

Yes, I am changed. I am made so much smaller than I ever thought I could be.

"Here it comes," says Hort, in my ear. He is there, I would swear it. I can still feel his hands on me but when I turn my head there is nothing beside me, and when I glance down at my limbs they are not there either. But I can feel them, their sinews stretching, my fingers and toes tingling with youth. "It's better if you see it, I think."

"See what?" I say, with my mouth that isn't there. I have a phantom body. And phantom emotions too, apparently, because I feel such love for the Earth at this moment even though I'm a reduction. But the Earth is my home, my magnet, my intimate friend that could never care for a speck such as myself. I am packed full of passion and gratitude for the continents before me – the bellyish curve of Africa that snakes upwards into Europe. The oceans, the visible and tactile juts of the mountain ranges, and the white blond tresses of the deserts: I want to worship them all.

But my Earth is not my god. It is living, and it can suffer.

The green. The dense, ugly green that destroyed my roses is blobbing into existence in so many places, spreading at an incredible rate, joining up to make a dense, interlocking mat that covers the world. The deserts, the forests, the oceans: gone to the uniform green. The cities begin to wink out, the fairy lights and cobweb patterns of humanity gone.

I can't comprehend it.

I think of Lily. Whatever she is experiencing right now cannot be rationalised or borne, and so I must try to find another level on which to process this loss.

I think of a flower.

The Lilium longiflorum is dying. Tall, over three feet high, with its creamy-white trumpeting blooms, facing up and out to the sun with those pure dots of pollen, strong yellow dust with a scent so sweet on display, open and brazen for bees and insects. Lilium longiflorum, native to the Ryukyu Islands of Japan which are dying too, toxic to cats which are also dying, once traded in vast numbers from Bermuda to the USA, both dying, and called the Easter Lily – consider the lilies, Jesus said, and the churches filled their vases with those long straight stems. The churches that are dying. Lilium longiflorum and all the things you mean –

you cannot die. You are my centre, and all the losses begin with you.

The vivid green that covers the Earth is changing colour. It's deepening, darkening. It's turning to a brownish black.

"I have the Collection and the Vice," says Hort, behind me now.

I cannot speak.

"Come on," he says. His voice is receding. "There is so much to do."

I would ask where, if I could bring myself to speak. Where is there to go? The most beautiful thing I ever saw is suffering before me. I have to bear witness, because I am so meaningless compared to it that any course of action is surely pointless.

I never should have left.

"Look at me."

I turn to him, swivelling in space, and he is not there. Instead there is only a dot of white light, vibrating very fast, blurring with the movement. "You can do this, Pea." I realise his voice is only in my head.

"My planet," I say. "I can't—"

"Not your planet any more. You're no longer human."

"How can we be speaking?"

"We're not speaking. These aren't words. You're processing it on those terms, for now. It will all begin to make sense to you, I promise. But right now we need to get home, so we can start finding a cure."

"Home?"

"My basement." He says *basement* in my head as he floats away, but I'm aware that he's not really saying that word at all. He's saying something much more complex. It's along the lines of *ingenious storage solution with interdimensional functionality*, but then my brain (which no longer exists) reasserts the meaning as *basement* with a touch of *greenhouse* thrown in, and in that state of confusion, despair and emptiness I do the only thing I can do.

I follow him.

We don't float far. His light stops, then veers, making straight lines with sharp right angles until he has created a rectangle. The darkness peels back from the top right corner; beyond it there is brilliant white. I feel a sucking sensation upon me, and I am being pulled into the hole. *Doorway*, translates my missing brain. *Possibility. Beginning. End.*

❭ • ❬

I can feel the edges of my awareness telling me that I'm not seeing what I'm seeing. I'm catching myself in the act of translation, making sense of impossible things.

I'm lying on a comfortable bed. Above me, stretching up into the dull sky, is a twisted spire of glass and metal that reaches so high it becomes hazy, indistinct to me, as if obscured by clouds.

I'm inside, right in the centre of a vast building. A cathedral made of glass. If this was a human accomplishment there would be so many people's hard work at which to marvel: architects, builders, teams of workers, and then a congregation to gather within it, faces turned up to that incredible spire, singing their sacred praises.

But no, this is Hort's home. No worship takes place here, unless he has private gods of his own.

It's an uncomfortable thought, one that leads to the realisation: *How very little I know about him.*

But at least, in this place, he is a man again. He is standing beside me, a man in flesh and form with his flyaway hair and his green lace-up shoes.

I get up from the bed and it sinks away, and disappears. Beneath the floor I see only dull grey sky. Perhaps we are flying.

I pat my hair, my stomach. I rub my elbows through my cardigan and my thighs through my casual trousers. I am not changed. I'm certainly not younger, judging by the wrinkles and dark veins decorating the backs of my hands. And not fitter, either, if the curves of my breasts and stomach are anything to go by. That's a shame, part of me thinks, but another part disagrees. It's good to be familiarly me. It might just keep me sane.

"What are you seeing?" Hort says, with a smile. I tell him. "Well, whatever works for you, I suppose."

"This is your greenhouse basement," I venture, even though there aren't any plants and we're obviously not underground. Looking through the panes of glass, each one an irregular crazy-paving kind of shape, I realise that there isn't sky outside either. There's only a grey space that stretches away. But at least that means I don't feel claustrophobic, I suppose.

"It's an ingenious storage solution in a location between other locations," he says, "but I call it home." For a moment, when I blink, I see complex textured folds in many jarring colours that make me flinch, but it passes. The bed has disappeared, though. The cathedral is no longer empty. Now it is truly a place of worship to something I understand.

Flowers.

There are flowers everywhere, growing up from the glass floor and out from the walls, curling and opening and closing as if living their lives on fast forward, and yet not wilting, fading or dying. They create, between them all, a scent so sweet and strong that tears form in my eyes. Blossoms intermingle impossibly; the Gazania of South Africa, with soft yellow petals that only unfurl in bright sunshine, grows next to a heap of Tufted Saxifrage, silky swaying balls that are found in the high Arctic. Earth's flowers have been somehow freed from the consideration of climate.

"This is what you were creating, you and your father before you," says Hort. "This is your Collection. I can access it, here. I can make it grow."

Behind the word *Collection* I hear *bank, safeguard, intensification, hope*, and *cemetery*. I smell, beneath the bouquet of the living blooms, the tang of decay. It's too much. I push it all away, try to make it one thing, and one thing only, in my head.

"Try not to fight it," murmurs Hort, but I must, I must keep all this information in a container I can hold. I concentrate on my flowers alone.

"How did you get them out of the discs?" I ask.

"They weren't ever really in the discs. They're composed of the same thing that I am. That we are, now. Information. That's what the Vice does, too. If only we could work out how your father got hold of that kind of technology. Where the Vice comes from. It can only be from an alien source."

"My father consorted with aliens?"

"Like father, like daughter," he says, and my thoughts move instantly to Lily. Where is the one flower I want to see? I search for it, through so many thousands, and when I look down at my feet it is right before me, where the Gazania grew. Lilium longiflorum: as tall as my thighs, the gentle curve of the creamy-white petals, its sweet scent. It is a perfection and an elegy.

Grief comes to me again. But thankfully, horribly, it is not utterly overwhelming. The edge of it is blunted. Hort was right. It's not going to cut me deeper than I can stand, because I'm not human any more.

Hort clears his throat. I get the feeling he's uncomfortable with my erupting emotions, as if they're leaking out of me to make an embarrassing puddle on his glass floor.

"Sorry," I say.

"Anyway, look, I've had a long hard poke around the Vice. I hope you don't mind, Pea, but I wanted to get cracking."

A suspicion comes to me. "How long was I asleep?"

"You weren't asleep. And time isn't a thing here. It doesn't move."

But I'm certain time has passed. Days, even weeks. Some indeterminate and unprocessable length of time. And if I wasn't asleep then what was happening during that time? If this is the space between dimensions, where did my consciousness go to while he examined the Vice?

"But you've had long enough to look at the Vice."

"I needed to do something," he says. "I get fractious if I'm on my own. I'm the kind of person who needs company. Plus, I got used to having you around, Pea. I like it. Those five days on Earth meant too much to me. They still do."

"This," I look around the glass cathedral, and the grey beyond, "is so amazing, but it looks like a lonely life to me."

"It's not a life," he says.

"Look, you're going to have to stop gainsaying everything I say, at least until I get used to this idea."

He raises my hand to his lips, and kisses my knuckles. "You're right. I'm sorry. But you are willing to get used to it?"

"I will try," I promise, because it seems so important to him, judging by the relief on his face. But the truth is that I don't have a choice.

"Great!" I get the sense of too many emotions to process. *Relief* and *disbelief* are underneath that one word, and many more things besides. "Then shall we get on with looking for answers? I think I've found a place to start."

He drops my hand and steps back. An ordinary table springs up between us, upon which sits the Vice. "Look," he says.

It's the same as always. It's a small lump of iron with a slot and a hole, and nothing much else about it.

"I don't see anything."

"Look with your new eyes."

"New eyes? I can't just—" But there it is; with a flicker my awareness mutates, and I see a latticework of orange string wrapped over and around the Vice in haphazard fashion. The string appears to be in one continuous strand.

"'I know a planet where they make a lot of orange string. I thought we might as well start there."

"Right. That's all we have to go on. The Vice is covered in invisible orange string and you know of a planet that makes orange string."

"Look," says Hort, "do you want to save the universe or not? Something tells me the Vice can help us stop the virus, and this could be a lead."

"Yes, but I don't understand how the Vice could have something to do with—"

"There are reasons. Just trust me. I don't want to blow your mind before it's even begun to expand to the possibilities."

He draws a rectangle with one finger and the room peels back to reveal black space beneath. It's like turning a page to him, creating this kind of doorway. I can't see how I'll ever understand any of this.

"Come on, then,'" he says. He holds out his hand.

I take it, and we're off.

LILY, **PLANTED**

Lily: We've started.

Graham: Already?

Lily: Are you speaking or am I speaking? Dad?

Graham: You do it. It's your idea.

Lily: Hello. Hello, I'm talking to anyone who is not under six feet of green sludge. Hello mountain dwellers and astronauts and top secret military installations. I hope all those conspiracy theories about organisations who are all ready for the end of the world are true.

Graham: Say this is an SOS, Lily, that's the important bit.

Lily: This isn't an SOS. We're okay. We have supplies, and a safe place. We can survive.

Graham: For now.

Lily: Yes, Dad, for now. Which is a lot more than most people, I'm guessing.

Graham: Of course. You're right. I'm sorry. Can we— Do you think we could be kind to each other? There's not really anything else, now. All that's left is kindness.

Lily: There's more than that. But it is important.

[Silence.]

Graham: That's my daughter. The teacher. Go on, go on. You're in charge.

Lily: We are trying to reach an important person. I know, there are millions of missing, displaced, unaccounted for people around the globe right now. You're going to have to believe me when I tell you that she needs to be found more than any of the others. It's not that she's part of our family that makes her important. This isn't about love. We don't even get on that well.

Graham: Getting off topic...

Lily: She's an expert in cataloguing,

classifying and understanding plants, and she has a collection of seeds that could restock the world. We could regrow everything, once this mess is over, and this disease has ended. And I do believe it will end. So you see, I'm not lying. She might be crucial to saving us all. She was meant to be here, in this house—

Graham: Middle of Dorset—

Lily: When we arrived. I don't understand why she's not here, and how she could have taken the entire seed collection with her.

Graham: You're sure it's not here somewhere?

Lily: Dad, it's enormous. It filled the whole basement. And now all the racks are empty. At least, the top half of the racks, that aren't under all the seeping green sludge.

Graham: Sludge that's still rising.

Lily: This cottage is on a hill. We will be fine. Let me finish. Listen, if you happen to have internet access and you find this message online, and you know Penelope Greensmith, or know of her whereabouts, please, please, let us know. I'll put my contact details below the video, or you can leave a comment. Please. It's urgent. My mother could save the world.

Graham: Surely your phone is running out of charge by now?

Lily: I've got a solar charger, I've told you already.

Graham: How are you going to put this on YouTube when there's no broadband?

Lily: Dad, just let me turn this off and we can argue about it later, okay? I'm thinking it might work if I—

TEARTHUMB

A robust shove between her shoulder blades, a bright rush, the delight of acceleration: Penelope closed her eyes and screamed, riding a roller coaster to a new world without planning, without preparation, without any idea of what awaited her there.

She expected a bang, but the sensation upon arrival was one of a light touchdown, like a landing at the hands of an experienced airline pilot. Still, Penelope looked down at her feet, expecting to see a great crater at the point of impact, or at the very least a dent.

She was standing upon smooth, undisturbed ground. A gentle curve led up to the steep slope of a fleshy hill that was speckled with prickly patches of black growth.

It resembled a giant chin.

"Are we on a person?" she said to Hort, who was right beside her; where else would he be? His presence was reassuring, and familiar: his smile, his clothes, his green shoes. He was the same. And her body was the same too. It was both a relief and a disappointment, to be a recognisable person.

Hort laughed.

"What?"

"It's all in the translation. No, we're not on a person."

"Aren't we going to look a bit out of place? To the locals? I thought we'd be in disguise."

"You are hilarious!" He shook his head. "We'll look right to each other, just as I look right to you. It's all in the mind. Expectations, preconceptions. You might start to see actual forms every now and again, I suppose. That can happen." The more she watched his mouth form words, the more obvious it became that the movements didn't match the sounds. "Okay. Here we go. String." Accompanying the word *string* were concepts of *delivery*, *packaging*, and *universally agreed rules of interstellar travel relating to inanimate objects.*

Hort had started walking up the hill.

"Wait, what did you say?"

"String. This direction. To get our bearings." She set off after him; he looked set on conquering the crest of the chin, and drove a hard pace.

It had happened again when he said *string.*

Universally agreed rules of interstellar travel.

It was an incredible, encompassing concept. Was it even close, in translation, in this business of myriad meanings, to what Hort was actually saying?

"There are universal rules about string?" she called after him.

"That's right. It's a very amazing product. I've always wanted to come here and see it being harvested, actually. We should start seeing the string fields once we crest this hill."

Hill. Growth. Naturally occurring contour. Body part.

It was impossible to ask questions and keep up with Hort at the same time. She wondered if it was deliberate.

She couldn't bear the thought that she was irritating him already, or holding him back, so she did her best to match his pace and was breathing hard by the time they reached the top.

The peak of the chin was flat, and the stubbled skin was harder underfoot. As soon as Hort stopped walking she bent over, her hands on her knees, and concentrated on getting air into her lungs. The air was warm and there never quite seemed to be enough of it; every breath left her dissatisfied, hurrying to take another.

"Great view," Hort said. "You okay?"

She nodded, and managed to stand up. The drop on the other side of the hill was vertiginous; they were high above rectangular fields, which stretched away for miles and in which grew orderly trees uniformly spaced. At first Penelope thought a strong wind must be blowing for the branches to sway as they did, but then she realised each branch swayed independently, making their own shapes and patterns. The trunks were implanted firmly in the ground, at least. They did not get up and move. But the branches, each one bearing an outcropping of expressive twigs, waved. They looked like human arms, topped with hands and fingers, and they were waving to each other.

Bright pink birds resembling flamingos stalked languidly between the trees, reaching up to take mouthfuls of the patchy orange foliage.

"It's fantastic," she said. It was beyond comprehension and yet it was knowable, and beautiful, and disturbing. How could it be all of these things? There were too many emotions to feel, too many words to apply. Something within her, a previously closed and bolted part of her mind, burst open and brought sound with it to a world that she had thought silent.

There was a distant, lazy hum that she would have categorised as mechanical, and above it a blanket of chirruping, a throbbing, charged sound reminiscent of cicadas in great numbers. But the temperature was mild, at best. So many aspects of this planet did not correlate. Being human involved an assumption that some things always went together, a sound to a vision, a texture to a smell.

Smell! Candyfloss. She breathed deep. Candyfloss, with the hint of a toffee apple to it. A fair, just like the one that used to come every September to the town in which she grew up.

A particular chirrup by her feet caught her attention. She looked down, and saw another familiar thing: a ladybird. It was bigger than the ones on Earth, perhaps ten times as large, and the shiny carapace was bright blue rather than fire-engine red. But the spots were the same, as were the white markings on a black face, and the jointed legs. She knelt, and put out her hand, palm down, in front of it. It extended a leg, and tentatively touched her.

"Really?" said Hort, who had been looking out over the view. "I wouldn't do that."

"Why not?"

"How do you know it's friendly?" She heard other words behind his voice – *docile* and *controllable* echoed there.

"How do you know it's not?" But the doubt, once placed in her mind, could not be erased. She backed away from the ladybird.

"Because you only see things as a reflection of Earth."

She stared hard at it.

It was still a ladybird.

She realised that she was squinting, treating it like a Magic Eye picture that only needed a different focus to allow the hidden image to surface. "I can't—"

The world – the sight and sound and smell of it – vanished.

Instead there was darkness all around, warm red darkness with flashes of strong heat on her face; a roaring sound, a sense of movement, huge things shifting their weight, nearby, exerting a pull on her; her arms lifted of their own accord. She forced them back down. Where was she?

The shapes began to coalesce into recognisable landmarks. The edge of the cliff was a space, a faded emptiness, and the trees were the source of heat, travelling at her in waves when the hands turned her way.

She looked down at her own hand. It was a river of energy, a pulsing yellow outline, cold. No fingers, no palm. Just a long, thin, curling stream like water flowing down to the ladybird, which was not a ladybird. It was not a creature, not in the sense she recognised. It was a hole in meaning, apart from the one thing about it that she could recognise as a mouth in its centre, from which jutted electric blue teeth at all angles. Liquid oozed from it, clear and viscose, and the mouth opened and closed with a smacking sound, like bare flesh being struck.

Her stream of energy was feeding it. She felt its enjoyment at the taste of her. She recoiled, and her stream snapped back automatically, away from its mouth. The waves of heat were coming at her in rolls; she realised they were no longer from the trees alone. She was creating heat, it poured from her in bursts. The mouth in the hole that had been a ladybird shrivelled under the force of it.

Panic overwhelmed her. She tried to take deep breaths, became acutely aware that she wasn't breathing at all. But she wanted to breathe, she wanted to breathe! She wanted the dark red world to leave her alone, for the familiar to return.

The heat was intense. It exploded from within her. Hort was saying something but she couldn't make sense of it, and then her awareness fragmented into many parts and words had no function any more. She was free, dissipated, like sycamore seeds spinning, caught in the wind. Her vision showed her all angles and all possibilities. She was light and she was limitless, and she wasn't Penelope any more, and parts of her were being carried out over the edge of the cliff, and the drop was so huge, she would fall she would fall she would fall she would fall

> • <

"Pea."

Penelope opened her eyes.

She had eyes again, in the traditional sense. And a body. And it was so heavy, so burdened by familiar complaints. Her feet hurt, for a start. She had a dry mouth, and sore knees. She felt human.

Hort's face, close above her, was a picture of sympathy. "You all right? You got a bit carried away."

"I was light."

"No, you weren't. You were a mess. You have to hold yourself together, Pea. I managed to round you up and put you all back this time. Listen, we've got important work to do here and we're running out of time. I need you. I need you to be on top of that. Stay in human terms, okay? It's not accurate, but it'll do well enough."

She realised she was lying flat on her back, in a room with an arched, ridged ceiling and thick walls formed from the trunks of the armlike trees she had seen earlier. The thought of someone cutting them down revolted her, but then she noticed how the curve of the roof and the doorway grew from the living substance, the branches interweaving, linking hands. Pinkish light slid through the gaps left between the trunks; they grew together to form a small covered space. A hut, it could be called. She watched the arm branches bend a little, stretch out, and the hands unlocked and wiggled fingers before resettling in different positions.

"Could you get up, do you think, Pea?"

She took his outstretched hand, mindful of how it mirrored the actions of the walls around her, and managed to stand even though her back and knees complained strongly.

"Well done. Listen, there are some people coming to see us. If you get asked, you come from the coast, okay?"

"From the coast?" That raised a hundred other questions, but she swallowed them all as a flamingo appeared in the doorway. Really, it did look exactly like a flamingo, even down to the knobbly joints of its legs and the long downwards sweep of its black beak.

"Who's this?" said the flamingo.

"She's with me," said Hort. "She's got an investment in this issue too."

"Is that right?" The flamingo turned its head to the side to fix one eye upon her.

"I'm from the coast," she said.

The flamingo assessed her, then refocused on Hort. The words had, apparently, worked. "You want access to formal records, you'll need a hell of a lot more than a few of us on your side, you know that, right? And you've given me no reason to believe you."

"You know who I am. You knew it as soon as you saw me. And you're desperate."

"That's not a reason."

"No," said Hort. "But it is a motivation."

The flamingo leaned all its weight on one foot, and tucked the other up inside its lower, dense feathers. "You've got an actual plan, I take it?"

"Get in, get what I need, hand over control to you on the way out."

"Ha! Funny. You're a wit."

"All my friends say so. Pea, this is Fluffy."

"Fluffy?"

"It's a family name," said Fluffy, and Penelope thought - *this isn't real, this isn't actually happening at all*. She was beginning to appreciate how her mind was making it bearable by substituting familiar things and words and actions for whatever was really taking place. The ladybird, for instance: she had made a ladybird of a thing so bizarre, so beyond her capability to process. She was very glad that she was dealing with Fluffy the flamingo, although she had to wonder exactly how she looked and sounded to it. A lot was probably being lost in translation.

"Are you ready? Time is of the essence," said Hort.

"I've got a small team together, just as you suggested. Ready to leave in an _____." No sound emerged from its beak; possibly it was describing a measure of time that had no human equivalent.

"We'll be here. All fired up and raring to go." Hort clapped his hands together.

Fluffy chuckled. "Raring to go. That's a good one. We're all going to die." It stalked out, bending its long, graceful neck to duck through the doorway.

Hort turned to her. "Right," he said. "You need to understand what's happening here, and that means we've got an awful lot of exposition to get through so I'll just ping that straight into your brain, if that's okay with you." The word *brain* came with a side order of meanings:

storage unit. human affectation. illusion of free will.

"I'm not sure what that would involve," she said. "I've been through a lot today and my feet really hurt."

He pulled gently at her hands until she stepped closer, close enough to be called intimate, to feel his breath on her nose and cheek. Was he breathing? Was she? Did it matter? If she never learned to see the reality of the universe, would it matter as long as the illusion was her friend?

"I've got so many questions," she whispered, and he put one finger to the centre of her forehead.

TEARTHUMB: Time of War
In a world of cruel injustice, the oppressed Flamingo rebels finally have the ability to strike back at their tyrannical overlords. Their only hope lies in taking over The Tower, the information hub that controls the sale and production of the planet's unique resource.

TIMETAPE

*The orange string found on the famed Limbtrees
of Tearthumb is the most expensive substance in
the universe, and remains shrouded in mystery. It
cannot be replicated in off-planet conditions; only
Timetape grown directly from Limbtrees retains
its ability to travel faster than light. Not only
that, wrapping it around other objects transports
them, enabling universal commerce.
A nomadic warlike tribe known as the Tyrants
has subjugated the peaceful Flamingos.
An uncaring universe has not intervened;
enslaved, the planet produces more tape than
ever before.
But now the Flamingo Rebels have a new and
powerful ally.*

THE HORTICULTURALIST

*The legendary and mysterious space traveller
has arrived on Tearthumb. Along with his plucky
assistant (pot plant) he means to enact his audacious
plan to return power to the unfairly oppressed.
His small band of helpers includes three brave
Flamingos, each with their own special ability, who
will risk all to help the Horticulturalist right the great
wrong that has been done to their people.
The time has come.
The time is now.*

"Wow," said Penelope, once her vision had cleared.

"Got all that?" Hort stepped back and smiled at her. "Good, huh? It makes things so much simpler."

"Tearthumb."

"Yep."

"It's a plant. An Earth plant. A climbing vine, in fact. Quite aggressive. I have a sample of it in my Collection."

"Really? So this whole enterprise is on the dangerous side, but you're up for that, right? Danger, excitement, thrills…" He wiggled his fingers. "Plus it's for an excellent cause."

"Yes, I can see that, and I don't want to sound churlish, but how does it help Earth? And the rest of the universe? How does it stop the virus?"

"Did I not cover that? Okay, well, this is a two birds with one stone kind of situation," he said, sitting down on the floor and crossing his legs. "The Tower contains records of all transactions in Timetape. Every single one. We know the Vice was transported to Earth at some point, where it was given to your father. Very few deliveries go to Earth, I'm betting, since it's a planet not covered by any universal trade agreements at present."

"All this stuff about universal trade. Are you saying there are people, creatures, in charge of the universe? A ruling body?"

He waved his hand. "Irrelevant, and far too complicated. Okay. To continue. We can find out who sent the Vice to Earth by checking the records, do you see? The Tyrants would never tell us, but if we put the Flamingos in charge they'll owe us a favour. Win win."

"That's very convenient."

"Sit down, Pea." He waited for her to kneel opposite him. All of her aches and pains had disappeared once more; they seemed to come and go depending on how many other things she had to think about. "Sometimes, very rarely, the good of the few and the many are the same thing. I should know. I've been at this game a long time."

"The legendary and mysterious space traveller," she repeated. "And his assistant, pot plant."

"You got called a pot plant? Must be a glitch. Do you meditate, at all? Fancy giving it a go? It can be handy in the business of keeping yourself together." He closed his eyes, and hummed.

Penelope felt his attention switch away from her. He could be so encompassing, so central to her well-being, but he could also remove those gifts in an instant simply by focusing his mind elsewhere.

It was a frightening realisation.

Still, all she could do was follow suit and try to meditate.

She had no idea what she was doing.

Thoughts, feelings, fears and doubts sprang up and assailed her in the blank space behind her closed eyelids. And there were more questions. Endless questions.

She diligently pushed them all away as they came to her and tried to find some peace on the fragmented, fantastical terms she had been given. The only thing that worked was an image of a lily. Lilium longiflorum. She built it painstakingly, one petal at a time, and it glowed for her, before her, around her. She realised she had built it from words that came together, combined, to form the flower. It was beautiful.

Lilium longiflorum. Japan. Easter. Daughter. Love. Petals. Scent. Anther. Ovary. Stamen. Sigma. Birth. Growth. Bloom. Style. Raising. Meaning. Happiness.

She kept at it as the time passed, and Hort put his energies elsewhere.

>•<

Three brave flamingos.

They stood in the hut, in a line. Penelope had never been so close to such large birds before; she felt nervous of them, as she would in the proximity of any wild animal. It was not a reaction that could be deprogrammed simply by noting its existence. Instead she opted to hide it. She got up from the floor, willing herself to look calm.

"This is Princess. Explosives."

It was a tall, elegant flamingo with a ruff of lighter, almost white, feathers around the base of its neck. It inclined its head with grace at the introduction Hort had provided.

"Tim. Theological expert."

Tim was shorter, with a kink to its neck that thrust its head forward at an odd angle. It nodded at Penelope.

"And you already know Fluffy, who helped build the Tower when the Tyrants first arrived. There's not a Flamingo alive today who knows more about that place."

"That's because they killed all the rest," said Fluffy.

"And you," said Princess. "What is your speciality?"

"I'm from the coast."

"Oh. Right." Princess shrugged at the other Flamingos, who were staring at it. "What? I didn't know."

"And you all know my name," said Hort, cheerfully. "Okay then. Off we go. I'll run through the plan on the way."

"I'd rather we discussed it now," said Fluffy.

"No time. Seriously, there's much less time than you think. Let's crack on. Do you have the ball?"

Fluffy lifted a wing. Tucked up in the dense, downy feathers of its armpit was a small ball of orange string. Timetape. Princess's and Tim's necks bowed low in what seemed to be an automatic reaction to the ball. "Don't make me regret using it on this mission." It refolded its wing, and the others straightened up.

"I won't." Hort crossed the hut to him, and patted his wing, above the Timetape. "I promise you. We share the same goals. We're going to make it better." He stepped past the Flamingos and out of the doorway of the hut. They all filed after him, and Penelope followed suit.

Time had passed, although it was difficult to say why she felt that way. Perhaps the sky was a little darker. The chirping sound was stronger, possibly, and the activity of the trees more energetic. Or was it a combination of all three? As it was on Earth, with that clear intensity of dusk, insects taking to the sky and the swallows swooping to catch them: night falling, like a pause, a breath of relief for the end of the day.

Hort had his back to them all, with his palm pressed against the trunk of a tree which paid him no attention in return. The limbtrees were busy reaching for each other, clasping and unclasping hands, groping for contact. Some of them bore remnants of orange string between their fingers, knotted around the knuckles, but most of the hands were totally bare. It came to her that the trees were, on some level, incredibly lonely. As if they were reaching for someone or something to connect with, but couldn't recognise what fellow beings surrounded it. How easy it would have been for a tree to reach down to Hort's hand and hold it, take comfort in it.

But the grasping – no, that was for something specific. The Timetape that had been harvested and taken away from it. Once Penelope thought of it, she couldn't imagine any other reason for Hort to touch it, to try to soothe it so. The trees imbued the landscape with a profound sadness, and suddenly this world was darker to her, and colder.

Hort turned from the tree. She saw tears on his cheeks.

"Let's go," he said.

They began walking. Penelope stayed at the back, following the direction of the others. Hort and Fluffy took the lead, striding ahead, deep in intense conversation, their heads close together. Tim and Princess did not speak, but seemed easy in their own silence.

There were so many naked trees, and every once in a while Penelope's attention was taken by a ring of them forming a hut. Without a door, she could see inside to get a glimpse of the flamingos that lived there. Work had, apparently, ceased for the time being. Families, friends, groups, had gathered together. Smaller birds had already tucked their heads under their wings. Tearthumb darkened again, the sky painted around the treetops now purple. Was she painting it? Was this, in some way, her world?

Hold it together, she told herself.

The thing was, what difference did it make? What possible difference could it make if she perceived this place on her own terms, using ideas from Earth to supplant a reality that she could not understand without losing herself in the process? The only thing that really mattered was stopping the virus. First up, that meant finding out where the Vice came from. All she had to do was keep that in mind, and aim for it.

And yet.

It was so very upsetting to think she was incapable of seeing difference properly. It would be pointless to travel a universe if all the sights, sounds and smells of it had to be filtered through the tiny pinhole camera of her own humanity in order to understand it in anything approaching human terms.

She was falling behind.

Penelope hurried to catch up with Tim and Princess, who draw apart to give her a space between them. It wasn't possible to fall into the loping rhythm of their thin legs, and if she watched the backwards bend of their joints for a few steps she found herself getting confused about how her knees worked, but she managed to keep pace.

"How did you meet him?" Tim asked her, jerking his head in Hort's direction.

"He arrived one day, unexpectedly."

"That is the nature of him."

"He's been good to me," said Penelope, carefully, wanting them both to be clear that she belonged with Hort, even when it came to casual conversations.

"Well of course," said Princess, as if any other treatment at his hands would be unthinkable.

"How did you know about him?" Penelope asked.

Tim coughed, then intoned, "The legend said he would come and end our oppression. It has been passed down from beak to beak for as long as the Tyrants have held us captive. We're honoured to be part of his coming."

Princess let out a deep hum.

"I'm honoured," Tim amended. "Princess thinks this is a set-up and Fluffy is reserving judgement. They are non-believers. That's okay, though. He's been a long time coming. The legend said it was fine to lose faith."

"Not having faith is okay?"

"Why would faith be needed when his coming was inevitable? Only those who don't intend to keep up their end of the bargain demand faith from those left waiting for it."

Penelope did not answer. It struck her as an unhuman (inhuman? Not exactly) sort of thought, perhaps the first proper Tearthumb thought she had come across.

"They don't believe yet that it's really him. The Horticulturalist."

Messiah. Last hope. Icon. Death. Rebirth. Collector. Higher being. Handsome stranger. Light. Energy. Unpredictability personified.

"Ouch," said Penelope. Hort's full name had set off a landslide of connections and permutations in her brain, causing an instant headache. It was as if Tim had shouted into a ravine and received a thousand echoes back, each one different yet the same. She struggled to hold them all inside her, but it hurt like heartburn. She stopped and bent over, her hands on her knees, trying to stay human.

"You okay?" asked Princess. "Should I call the Horticulturalist?"

The reverberation of so many ideas and meanings, all encapsulated in one name: "Don't say it. Don't say it again," she begged, putting her hands to her ears although it would make no difference. Tim and Princess flanked her, and waited. Eventually the echoes receded enough to allow her to straighten up.

"Can you go on?" said Tim.

"Yes, I'm fine. Yes." She started to walk again, aware of the flamingos exchanging looks over her head. She was unreliable in their eyes, no doubt. A liability. She had to try harder.

They walked on, giving Hort and Fluffy their distance to make their plans. There was always somebody in charge of others, Penelope noted. The scrolling exposition had suggested the flamingos were fighting for a fairer system, but there were only three of them taking direct action, and only one was giving orders. The problem of deciding exactly what was fair and what needed to be done: had any planet solved it? Could it be solved?

The vast plains of limbtrees continued onwards, providing a welcome consistency. Occasionally the chirruping she had first heard upon her arrival on Tearthumb grew louder, close by, and she could pinpoint it to a particular branch. After passing a particularly vigorous chorus, Princess said to her, "The Buttons are mourning the loss of their string. Nobody will get much sleep tonight. Do you know about this? On the coast?"

"No. No, we know very little about the string."

"You have your own problems there."

Penelope hesitated, then said, "Don't we all?"

Tim, on her other side, said, "The Buttons are too small to see, but we know they are there. They take the liquid that the trees weep from their palms, and they spin it into strings, forming elaborate patterns. When we harvest it for Timetape the Buttons are loud in their sorrow. All that hard work taken away from them. They will cry themselves to sleep soon, and then lie dormant for the season of rest. This time is known as the Long Night of Loss. It's a holy night. The Tyrants will never expect an attack. It's perfect timing. It's also an affront to the Great Weaver."

"Oh give it a rest," said Princess.

"I'm here, aren't I? I'm taking part."

"With your holier-than-thou attitude in place, yes."

"It's what I believe! It's what we were both brought up to believe, and just because you've dumped it in order to look cool, doesn't mean I should too."

"You really want to fight about this right now? You are so like Mother."

"Don't," said Tim, "say I'm like Mother. Just don't even go there."

"You're siblings," said Penelope.

"We're what?" They paused in their bickering; the word was unfamiliar to them, perhaps. She tried again.

"You were raised from the same clutch of eggs?"

"Of course. Why else did you think we looked so similar?"

"Yes, I can see it now," she said, although in truth they all looked the same to her.

That thought brought back an uncomfortable memory of her grandmother from when she was little; so little that it was framed in her mind as a crystallized, complete moment, floating in still time. It was the anchor of her entire relationship with her grandmother, all she thought of when the woman came to mind, and it centred around toast.

A slice of hot white toast, pooling butter, served to her on a thin white plate to hold on her knees while she ate sitting in front of the television, legs swinging from the armchair. Her father would have been busy with the Collection, as usual. She was watching a children's programme, and two presenters, a man and a woman, were smiling at her from the screen while they made a model from yogurt pots and a wire coat hanger (a memory of annoyance always accompanied this – why did her father not eat yogurt? Where was she meant to get these pots when opportunity never presented itself?). And her grandmother said, while handing her the plate, *Which two are these? Never mind, they all look the same to me.*

The comment, viewed through the telescope of time, had taken on so many sinister layers of meaning later. Did television presenters all look the same? Or had she referred to the colour of their skin? Or the length of their hair, or the cut of their clothes? It had become, over the years, Penelope's benchmark of casual discrimination without ever really being more than an ephemeral approximation of it. Funny, how it meant something so different to her that it could have ever possibly to meant to one old woman who made a lot of toast for a surly granddaughter.

And now, here she was, literally unable to see the differences between people (People? Yes, she was going to call them people, she decided) because she did not have the eyes for it. It was beyond her understanding.

Try harder, said her inner bio-librarian, who delighted in the recognition and categorisation of all things. But, for the first time, the danger of trying to observe the truth was obvious to her. She dared not risk it. No more Magic Eye diversions. It would only slow down the mission.

"Look," said Tim.

They were emerging from the orchards, and the last of the limbtrees gave way to a plains plunging down, rolling away from them, with the black stubble springing up to form wiry hairs, obscuring the fleshy ground under a bushy beard. Penelope's eyes were drawn to a path into the valley that had been formed by the plaiting of these long hairs along a lumpy seam, like a scar. The path steepened as it fell into darkness; as they followed it further the smell of candyfloss grew stronger.

Hort and Fluffy stopped walking and waited until Penelope and the others caught up. Hort gave her a smile that calmed her churning thoughts a little.

You can do this, she told herself.

"You okay?" he asked, then said, "This leads to the Tower. It's not far now. We need to look pious. Can you keep your wingtips together and your eyes on the ground?"

"Ummmm…" She clasped her hands and tilted her chin downwards.

"Perfect. Tim, you lead the way. We might see guards from this point in. If that happens, let Tim do the talking."

Tim stepped forward, assumed the position of piety, which involved an uncomfortable looking bend of the neck, and began a stately, stalking walk forward.

"You next, Pea. I'll walk close behind you. Princess next, then Fluffy at the rear."

She did as she was told, keeping her gaze on the seam of the beard, aware of Hort behind her. How closely the strands of black hair were plaited. It must have taken so many workers to complete this route; what a huge task it must have been. She had no doubt that the flamingos had done it while the Tyrants looked on, but that was the nature of oppression, of course. It was easy to picture whips, desperation and screaming. If flamingos could scream.

The smell of the fair increased; it was strong, and unwanted. It brought back another memory that she would rather have forgotten.

I want a goldfish, she had said to her father.

Will you look after it?

All those clear plastic bags, pinched and tied at the top, arranged in rows along the sides of the booth: each one containing a shiny golden fish.

Three Balls for 50p.

Could her father win one? Of course he could, with his clear aim and strong arm. That was never in doubt.

Choose one, then.

They all look the same, said her inner voice, across time, across worlds. Had she thought that at the time, or was she injecting the present into the past? But no, it wasn't true, there was a goldfish that was unique: third row, fourth along, with skin grown over where an eye should be. It was swimming askew, tilted to one side, the eyeless side turned upwards to the seal of the bag as it made its circles.

That one.

She called it Goldie and, for all her delight with it, it was dead in the morning. She had wallowed in this first heartbreak. Perhaps she had sensed that would be the outcome and that was why she had chosen it. To love for the difference, the uniqueness, even though it meant it could not last. Because it meant it could not last.

Candyfloss smell, go away, she thought. *Go away, go away*, in time to her steps, over and over.

The ground continued to slope down and the darkness around them deepened until the brightest thing by far was the white stripe of the seam they walked along. She did not raise her head at all, not for a moment. Hort's statement that they were possibly being watched was stuck in her brain; she could not risk jeopardising the mission.

The crying of the Buttons faded away, and a new sound took its place - a thin, high whine, not constant, but at regular intervals, coming from somewhere overhead. It put her teeth on edge. Her peripheral vision told her nothing; the sides of the valley through which they walked were steep, and the path fluoresced. She wondered if the hairs had all been plaited by hand. What a huge task that must have been, and entirely in the nature of slavery as she understood it. The many creating incredible things because the alternative was pain or death. It was profoundly depressing to think such problems had not been solved on other planets, and that cruelty was not a singularly human characteristic.

The whine grew louder and louder.

"We're nearly there," said Hort, by her right ear. She realised he had caught up to her, and felt a profound relief to have him close again. "Let's do it. Tim, you're up."

Everyone came to a stop. Tim bowed its long neck so that its beak was nearly touching the ground. Then it lifted its wings slightly, just enough to create a hollow in the spot where its neck met its body creating a perfectly round depression into which Fluffy placed the ball of Timetape it had been carrying. It could not have been a heavy object, but Tim shuddered, and let out a long sigh.

Walking resumed, Tim in front holding that uncomfortable position, moving carefully. Penelope watched Princess's and

Fluffy's deference as they moved off. Princess may have claimed to be irreligious, but the sense of ceremony was still strong within the group.

She fell into step.

Down into the valley once more.

The seam veered sharply, leading to a small stretch of flat hairless ground that narrowed into a strip between two expanses of russet-coloured swamp, from which came small eruptions of hissing air, making her flinch. Was it safe to look up? What would she see? Tim came to an abrupt halt and the strip widened and hardened into something familiar, like stone. The candyfloss smell was so strong it took on a metallic edge.

She couldn't help it. She glanced up.

They were at the foot of a huge white building. It was enormous, conical, like a giant helter-skelter in appearance. And it was topped with a spire far above, tapering to a barely visible needle, but they had walked so deep into the valley that it was barely higher than the sides of the perfectly round bowl in which it sat. This wasn't a natural valley at all, but more evidence of hard labour; the land itself must have been cut to this shape. The high whine returned, and the tip of the spire flashed out an orange spark, up into the air and gone into the ether.

It had to be the Tower.

"Head down!" muttered Hort.

"Sorry." She kept her eyes to the ground once more as they made their final approach to the Tower. She was aware that she had managed to take in only a few details of what surrounded her. If it had been possible, she could have stared for hours, and yet felt come no closer to understanding this place.

Penelope nearly walked into the back of Fluffy as the group came to a sudden halt, but she managed to pull up short just in time.

"The Buttons cry," intoned Tim. "The Limbs mourn. The Tape ends. It will spool forth again."

"District?" said a coarse, croaky voice. It pronounced the word strangely, with the stress on the first syllable.

"Plenty Hills."

"You're early."

Tim did not reply. The silence stretched on. She wanted to look. If only she could look.

"The Buttons cry," Tim said. "The Limbs—"

"All right, all right, don't get your ceremonial ball in a knot. Follow me." There was a snigger, on the left. A different position. There were at least two of them, then. "Come on!"

She dared to sneak a peek at the feet of the one remaining in place as they passed through the opening of the Tower. Boots. Silvery boots, completely enclosing the feet within. Were the Tyrants completely clad in the stuff? Or were they made of it?

Were they robots?

Robot space warriors: the thought scared her more than the idea of an animal adversary. Such things could not be swayed by emotion, or empathy. Surely there was nothing worse than a hard, unyielding robot foe. And yet their interaction with Tim suggested a sense of humour. A cruel one, but a sense of humour nonetheless.

The white floor was marbled with purplish veins, visible in a light from some diffuse source overhead that also warmed her. She risked a quick glance ahead; the walls were of the same material, and the corridor curved away to the left in a gradual arc, sloping downwards. The view of the back of the Tyrant showed a suit of metal to match the feet, half as tall again as the flamingos and twice as wide. Humanoid in shape, and very shiny.

They walked on, and the corridor curled around and down. Underground. Penelope felt her fear intensify; surely a Tower should require ascension? Seeing it, from the outside, she had assumed they would be climbing steps to a lofty goal. But no, down, in a circle, and still she could not see where the light was coming from. It could have vanished at any moment.

Into the depths of the Tower, every step a challenge. Then, eventually:

"In here."

There was no pause in their walking. The guard fell back, watched them pass. Penelope felt a gaze upon her, and then she was past and breathing out, before slamming into the back of Fluffy, who had come to a halt along with the others.

It was a tiny room. A cell, really, with only one furnishing in the shape of a long rug composed of tough green fibres that reminded Penelope of plastic.

"You wait," said the guard.

The terror of being locked in such a small space, pressed close to the others, overwhelmed her. She pushed forward, heading for the corridor once more, but the sight of the guard stopped her in her tracks.

The metal plates of its helmet were opening. They folded outwards from the centre, where a human nose might sit. It was like watching a flower open, but inside was no flower. Eyes. Eight of them: lidded, yellow, with black pupils that narrowed to slits. Four mouths. Set in four different heads. Lizard heads.

The heads, two on top, resting their chins on the scaled foreheads of the two below, had that sharp, malevolent look to them that Penelope associated with the dinosaurs she had once seen in a blockbuster movie. Velociraptors, was the name that came to mind. Intelligent, voracious predators.

It spoke. Only the lower left mouth spoke; the other mouths stayed shut.

"Problem?" it said.

Should she say she was from the coast? Tim, coming to the front of the cell to stand beside her, came to her rescue. "Forgive, forgive. A new one. A young one, in awe of you."

The Tyrant's visor began to close, pinching together. "It eyeballs me again, it dies." The visor snapped together. Then it moved away.

There was no door clanging shut, no barrier descending to stop them from leaving the room. And yet the flamingos and Hort began to settle themselves, with Hort sitting cross-legged on the rug while Tim tilted forwards to allow the Timetape to roll from its position on its back to the ground.

"What now?" said Penelope, as quietly as she could.

Fluffy's head was already tucked under its wing, and one leg tucked away in preparation for sleep. Its muffled reply was not a surprising one.

"Now we wait," it said.

> • <

Saving the world involved a lot of waiting.

It was surprising to Penelope how fear and incomprehension, mixed in vast amounts, produced such tiredness. The simple act of closing her eyes would have taken her into sleep beyond interruption, but she dared not let go in such a way. What if she broke apart into a thousand tiny pieces again? It couldn't be risked. So she sat down beside Hort, with his eyes closed, his body relaxed, his hands on his knees, wrists bared – a classic image of repose – and whispered, "How long?"

"It's all relative," he said. "Don't worry. Everything's under control. You're doing incredibly well."

"Am I? I can't even begin to describe how ridiculous everything looks to me. It reminds me of a trip I took to the zoo with my father when I was eight or nine."

He opened his eyes, and gave her a wink. "You know, it's okay for saving the universe to also be fun."

"You think this is fun?"

"I'll let you into a secret." He leaned in close. "You don't have a body. You can't actually be killed. Does that help?"

"Umm..."

"Have a think about it, okay?" He touched his shoulder to hers, then closed his eyes and returned to meditation.

Other flamingos arrived regularly. They walked past the doorway in the familiar position of religious humility, led by a Tyrant guard in full armour every time. The fear was so real, coursing through her. Terror: a hormonal response, surely? It couldn't be happening to a woman without hormones.

Thinking about these things did her no good; how could any answers be forthcoming when there was no logical starting point to extrapolate from? But she thought about it anyway, and found herself wishing for sleep, Earth and familiarity.

Adventure was exhausting.

If this had been a film (one of those with a bit of mild peril) then this dull moment would have been cut. It was the black screen between set pieces – the space of the cut from frame to frame. Into this blankness, this absence of action, memories kept pouring. Every moment, every smell, reminded her of something from home, from the past. Were *home* and *the past* the same thing? Were those words about to meld? Meanings were so slippery, subjective, circumspect, suspicious.

She couldn't trust words any more.

It was a horrible business, waiting, particularly en masse. More and more flamingos arrived and were led to their own cells, she supposed. She could feel time as a weight upon them all. The weight of waiting.

Behave, words. Words, behave.

She let out a long sigh, half hoping Hort would stir, talk to her again, but it was Princess who unfolded her long neck, fluffed out her ruff, and stalked over. Penelope stood up, to make the height difference less incongruous.

"Unbearable," whispered Princess.

"You hate waiting too?"

"For things like this, yes. Not that I've done anything like this before."

"Will it be much longer?"

"_____" said Princess.

"Pardon?"

"_____"

"I can't—"

"_____. _____ _____." Princess was changing colour, from pink to a deeper red, then on to a muddy, swirling brown, and her neck was thickening, elongating, squashing, which way was it moving? No, it wasn't moving at all. Penelope's own eyes were shifting in her head, except she had no head, and the floor was subsiding, collapsing into a pit, concave that flipped convex to become the crater of a rumbling volcano, the heat intense and awash, and the energy of it was building, building, for some great outpouring of meaning, of matter, of

"I've got this," said Hort, so close, into her ear that was not there, ear to brain, each sound signal

significance signatory circumvention

Tearthumb: The Rejoicing

And so the intrepid band of rebels, under the leadership of the one and only Horticulturalist with his faithful yet scatty assistant (pot plant) Pea, enacted their brave plan, and the Tyrants were forced to cede control of the Timetape to the flamingos once more.

One lone band had proved they could stand against the might of the oppressors.

As word of their victory spread, so the rebellion quickened, and soon the Tyrants threw down their weapons and retreated, in their ships, to dark space where they could regroup.

No doubt they would emerge again at some future time, on the hunt for another peaceful civilization to subjugate, for such villains are never truly defeated for long.

They return to test the true, over and over again.

*And **THE HORTICULTURALIST** will forever stand against them.*

But for now, it was time for the flamingos to mourn their losses.

The names of the fallen would never be forgotten...

> • <

A view.

Such a view, over the strange orchards of Tearthumb to the protuberant pink growths beyond, majestic mountains rising high, with the limbtrees as small as seedlings, swaying and reaching for each other, and the black stubble of the land forming patchworks.

At first it seemed to Penelope that she was floating above the world, but then sensation returned, and she felt a hard surface under her feet and a hot breeze in her hair. Even up here the sweet, sweet smell of candyfloss was strong.

Fear.

An awareness of height, of being able to fall, swamped all details; she reached out, clutching, trying to stabilise herself, and grasped—

Hort.

"You're safe," he said.

She held on to the material of his shirt as he put his arms around her.

"We're at the top of the Tower, that's all. Everything's fine. Everything's brilliant, in fact. We won."

Penelope, steadied, looked around. They were standing on a circular metallic platform, through which jutted a central tapered spike that ended four or five metres above them. At its lowest point, a small curved panel was set into the spike, into which was set a range of blinking red lights. Princess was there, tapping the lights with her beak in a blur of precise motions, her neck bent low while her torso was at the height of Hort's waist.

"What's happening now?" said Penelope. Her voice sounded surprisingly normal, but her hands wouldn't unclench from Hort's shirt. She had never liked heights. She couldn't die, but she could still fall. The thought was dizzying.

"The funerals have begun," said Hort. He didn't seem to mind the grip she had on him. "It's going to take some time. I'm afraid we can't wait around for them to finish the customary rituals. Princess very kindly agreed to find the information we need straight away, as per our deal. I do feel terrible about it, but our need is absolutely urgent."

Princess stopped tapping and straightened up. "It's okay. It's all religious bullshit anyway. I'll start phasing it out as soon as things are under control."

"Right, well, crack on then, please," said Hort.

Princess resumed tapping.

"Princess has been appointed First Minister in the new governmental system. She is, after all, the only surviving member of the Freedom Three."

"The Freedom... Wait, Fluffy? Tim?"

"Fluffy united the other delegations with a speech that was so incredible," Hort told her. "Really, hugely inspiring stuff. They all agreed to take up the cause. He led the first charge, which meant he was one of the first to fall. And Tim. Tim sacrificed himself. He threw himself into the path of a crack unit of Tyrants so we had the time to seal ourselves in the production headquarters and threaten to destroy it unless they co-operated. He's a martyr."

"It's what he always wanted," said Princess, mid-peck.

Penelope had never had a sibling, but loss – loss had a name to her. *Lily.* No matter what she could ever say on the subject of her daughter, or if she never spoke of it again, it would be inside her. She managed to disentangle herself from Hort and take the steps to Princess's side so she could lay a hand on the brittle, long feathers of her upper wing. "I'm so sorry," she said.

Princess paused, and said, "Thanks. He was the best of us."

"He was no more or less than what he was. He was unique."

"He was," said Princess, softly, and turned her head to nuzzle Penelope's fingers. "That's a very good description of him. Right, I've double-checked this. It's weird. There's no record of a Timetape transaction to this Earth place. It's not even on the trade lists."

"Are you absolutely sure?"

"I said I double-checked."

"Right," Hort said. "Well. Well then."

"There must be some mistake," said Penelope. "We know that—"

"I'm so sorry," Hort interrupted, "but we have to go. We'll say goodbye now."

"Right now?" said Princess. "We were going to have a medal-giving ceremony in your honour."

"No, no need. No medals. Listen, all the best. You can scoot off. We can take it from here."

"Don't you need to return to a ship, or—"

"No, no." He shooed her with his hands. "Listen, you were brilliant. I'm so glad this all worked out for the best."

"Yeah." Princess fluffed up her outer feathers. "Bye then, Pea."

"Bye," said Penelope, reluctant to let go of the moment, and the idea of the celebration to come. They were heroes. She'd never been a hero before, even if she hadn't actually been present in any recognisable sense for the heroic parts.

Princess took a few steps to the edge of the platform and launched herself off, into lazy, graceful flight, wheeling round and round, dropping in height, until she was out of sight.

"Ready to go?" said Hort. How tense he looked; the muscles in his cheeks were clenched. Somehow it made him look younger. He pointed, past her head. She turned, followed the line of his finger, and saw it: a vivid green carpet oozing over the black stubble of the hills, creeping up the limbtrees, melting the clutching hands away.

"No," she said. "No. It can't be."

"It moves fast."

"Why here? Why now?"

"Funny," he mused. "You never asked that question about Earth."

It was swallowing up an entire culture that she hadn't even begun to understand. Many cultures. So many plants, and people, and ways of being. She should have tried harder to make sense of it all, to bear witness. She needed this world not to end like this.

"We've got no answers," she said.

"We have! Pea, we can still save this planet too. I know who sent the Vice to your father."

"There were no records."

"Trust me, Pea!"

"I do, but... I do."

She watched him draw a large rectangle with his finger, and then a mighty shove from behind sent her falling through the doorway; the world turned black, and the warmth of blood or sun or something was on her face, she wasn't ready, she wanted to stay, and then she no longer had a face at all

LILY, BUDDING

Lily: Mum, are you there?

[Pause.]

Lily: I know this is ridiculous,
      but I... My name is Lily
      Greensmith and I'm looking for
      my mother. Her name is Penelope.
      She's about five feet and
      four inches tall, and she's
      plump, and has a strong chin.
      She wears a lot of cardigans.
      You'd know her if you met her.
      She talks about flowers. That's
      her major concern in life. If
      she's alive.

[Pause.]

Lily: When you want to speak to
      somebody, anybody, to the entire
      world, you use your phone,

right? That's what you do. You put out a message. This is my message, recorded in the middle of a sleepless night, through desperation I can't begin to describe. And yet this message has nowhere to go. There is no internet any more. I can't answer any of my questions, either. I'm used to instant gratification – think it, ask it, get a reply. If Google was still speaking to me, I would ask: why are we all not dead already? How are we still breathing? Plants take carbon dioxide and turn it to oxygen, correct? When there's only a swamp where there was once plant life, how are we surviving? I don't understand it. Maybe plants under the sea are still alive. Could that be it? Would that create enough oxygen?

[Pause.]

Lily: Mum would know.

[Pause.]

Lily: We're okay, though. We're okay.
       I feel strong, really. Calm
       inside. And Dad's doing well,
       too. We're observing the swamp
       and have been experimenting
       on samples, seeing how it
       reacts to different stimuli,
       fire, cold, acid, and so on. The
       result so far is: it doesn't. It
       might be pointless but it
       keeps us both busy. I think the
       alcohol test was a high point.
       Dad had grabbed everything from
       his fridge before we drove down
       here, and that included some
       cans of beer. He said, Who
       knows? Maybe beer really is
       the answer, and we cracked some
       cans and poured it over a
       sample. Of course, nothing
       happened, but drinking those
       cans of horrible warm Budweiser
       with Dad, giggling for the
       relief of still breathing, was
       so good. One of the best
       moments of my life.

                [Pause.]

Lily: I miss you, Kieran. I still
       can't believe it. I haven't

begun to make sense of it. I
wonder if there will be time to
make sense of it. Look at me,
videoing myself with no make-up,
in a pair of my mother's pyjamas,
speaking to my phone, pretending
to be making contact with the
entire of the rest of this huge
planet when the truth is I'm just
talking to myself. Mum, if you're
out there, with the Collection,
trying to save us, then get on
with it. I want to be saved. I
want time to mourn, and feel
terrible, and even consider
topping myself, sometimes. I want
the opportunity to have PTSD.

[Pause.]

Lily: The fact that the Collection
is gone must mean something.
She would never leave it. That's
not who she is. If I know her,
I know that's not who she is.
Graham: Are you okay?
Lily: I'm sorry, I thought you were
asleep, I was just... Hang on
while I turn this off.
Graham: What are you doing, sweetheart?
I really don't think...

ORDER

Plants, animals, gases, liquids, minerals, metals: forms of existence that I can categorise. They are a way to divide and conquer every object I might feasibly come across, on whatever planet. It doesn't matter if these are false categorisations as long as they continue to make sense to me. I have to remember that when the barriers start to waver, when the smells take on shapes, when my thoughts become motes, and scatter me far and wide.

I've been lying on this bed for a time. I don't know how much time.

Time:

age amount growth change perspective accumulation diminution

Stop stop stop.

I have keep an eye on language, too. I can't get lost down the alleyways of meaning that continue to open wide in front of me, force me to split apart and walk their routes. I have to remain human. Words must obey me. They must be pinned down, forced into boxes.

You don't speak to please yourself, Penelope Greensmith. You speak to communicate effectively with others.

I once had a teacher – not an English teacher, her subject was geography, which makes sense now I think about it – who reprimanded me with those words during a presentation I was giving to the class on the subject of tectonic plates.

The plates are shifting all the time, I said, to a spread of bland, uninterested faces on a sticky summer afternoon, the row of windows at the back of the room shut tight. *Although it feels like we're on solid ground, we can't trust the earth to stay still. It's lying to us. The land itself is mendacious.*

Stop, said the teacher. Mrs Franklin. Mrs Frankwell? Students called her Mrs Frankenstein, I remember that. It was something to do with the walk, the haircut.

Mendacious. She struggled to say it. *Tell me what that word means.*

I was stunned. How could a teacher not know a word? Teachers knew everything, and so I couldn't dream of explaining it to her. She took my silence for confirmation that I didn't understand the word either, and had been doing my best to sound impressive.

I had been attempting to sound impressive, of course, but I rather thought that was the point of school. I was undergoing a test, running a daily race that promised a reward. I had somehow failed that test for using a long word. I needed to prove I had acquired knowledge, but it dawned on me at that moment that I needed to do it without ever looking as if I was showing off.

You speak to communicate effectively with others. Why use a long word when a short word will do?

Mendacious has a specific meaning. It is thick and slippery, sour cream in the mouth. I could explain it in ten or so short words, talking around it to put up signposts that point to it as a destination: south of untrustworthy, east of fickle. But there will come a sentence where only that one word is true. It will be the right word. It feels like no other.

I believe this. Words can be true. They don't all have a myriad of meanings in all sorts of situations. Is the ground moving? The bed feels stable, but the tectonic plates are mendacious.

"Pea."

Hort is here, standing a few feet away, waist deep in white poppies: Papaver somniferum. My name clangs like a cymbal, and in its reverberations I hear so many things:

companion friend enabler remnant distraction pot plant

"How long have I been out?"

He shrugs. It's not a question he can answer, I remember. "Okay. Never mind. I'm back now. I'm myself again. What's the next move? We can still save Earth, and Tearthumb, right? I can't believe how quickly the virus reached—"

"Okay, calm down. I need you focused. There's only ever been one source of unregistered Timetape transactions. And that's the stolen spool."

"A stolen spool?"

"*The* stolen spool. The one time somebody managed to get off-planet with some of that orange string stuff that makes the universe go round. So we go see the thief, and we ask them, why did you use that string to send a strange contraption like the Vice to Earth?"

"We just turn up, and ask him? Her? Them?"

"Yep. Can you get up? Are you ready to travel?"

"I'm fine," I tell him, and try to make it true by getting off the bed and not falling over. I plant my feet on a freshly erupted patch of good English lawn, weed free. The grass variety is red fescue.

"Brilliant!" Hort, enthusiastic, is hard to resist. "Off we go. Except there's an item I really must collect first." The bed, the grass, the poppies, all shrink away into the glass walls and floor, and we're left standing in a plain space, with that strange grey skyscape beyond that could so easily be mistaken for clouds.

I can't help it. I feel nervous. "What if the next planet makes even less sense than the last? I can't seem to control words any more."

He takes my hands in his. "Stop thinking inwards, Pea. It'll do you no good. This is an adventure. Adventures travel outwards, not in." His eyes are so warm, so encompassing, and untouched by time or confusion. "Right. This way."

He doesn't move. Instead the walls and floor move to the left, and a whole new room slides in from the right, demarcated by a white strip. It's like reading a new panel in a comic strip; the place and time have changed and we are in a fresh box, drawn to meet a set of unspoken rules that all readers understand.

Hort faces the new room, so I do too. It's a dark, claustrophobic cube without doors or windows. I risk a glance behind and see the fourth wall has formed. The surface is grey and unmarked. Wooden racks fill up the small space. They are suspended from the low ceiling and don't touch the floor, and on the racks are so many small objects, cluttered together. It's like a junk shop, or the cave of some old hoarder, except it doesn't have that musty tang of age and accumulation.

"My stuff," says Hort.

The objects don't make any sense. Every time I shift my gaze to a new shelf, I get the sense that everything I just stopped looking at is rearranging itself. When I look again, nothing is familiar. How is this akin to my Collection? Things have not been placed with care. Nothing laid down in this space could easily be picked up again.

It reminds me of a quote I first came across while studying to become a librarian, back in the early days of the world wide web when we were only beginning to suspect that limitless potentials would lead to endless confusions. I liked it so much, at the time, that I memorised it, although the name of the writer won't come to mind, oddly enough:

'The current state of the internet can be likened to a library in which everyone in the community has donated a book and tossed it into the middle of the library floor.'

This Collection is not a library. It's a mess of continually changing trinkets. I see a rock, a horn, a shield. A single pink feather – did Hort take that from Tearthumb? How does he find order here, or does that not matter to him?

He puts his hands to the shelf closest to him, shoulder height, and touches the items there with gentle fingers, skimming, just like he did when he first visited my basement. There's no dust this time for him to pick up; dust is a human thing.

"Look!" he says. "Your Collection!" He takes down a plain cardboard box and opens the flaps. "Go on. Put your hand in."

I reach in, and feel a disc. Just one. I pull it out and press the button on the top, and am rewarded with a rotating 3D image: the unmistakeable sight and scent of Cosmos atrosanguineus, known as Chocolate Cosmos, a native to Mexico but extinct in the wild. Now extinct everywhere, I remind myself.

"Where are the other discs?"

"They're all in there! Amazing, isn't it? I made lots of these little boxes for general storage purposes. They come in very handy."

I put my hand back in, and pull out another disc. Another. He's right; they're all in there, somehow.

"I picture a box, and then I sort of push and pull it into existing," he says. "And anything that's in the Storage Room can be recreated, in as good as a solid form, in the Main Room."

"How?"

He shrugs. "It's really complicated. Not worth try to explain. I knew you'd like this place, though. Now, I need that thing."

Low down, on my right, I catch a glimpse of the Vice and turn my head to it. Yes, there it is, with orange string still visible. It sits beside a red plastic two-pronged fork, a miniature model of an octopus with translucent metallic wings on its head, a crumpled piece of yellow material that forms stiff peaks and folds, and a glinting nugget of something that might be gold except it keeps breaking down into a puddle and then pulling itself back together again.

And another of Hort's cardboard boxes.

"You've found it!" says Hort. "Clever you. Grab it for me, then."

I retrieve the box and pass it to him. How does he tell them apart? It looks the same as the first.

"You've got a knack for this place, Pea. I suppose I should have expected that, given your talents."

"I don't know how I did it," I tell him.

"Right then," he says. He puts the box up his shirt sleeve and it disappears; yet another trick I wish I had the hang of.

"Let's go get some answers. Remember, deep breaths if you feel yourself breaking apart. You're not really breathing, of course, but that doesn't matter."

"I wish you hadn't said that."

"Sorry."

"Wait, where are we going this time? Is there anything I should know?" But he's already drawing the rectangle with his finger and the space is glowing white, and then there's an almighty shove on my back and I'm falling once more, through and down and up and

CASTLEWELLAN

Prison Planet!
Hort, intrepid explorer on a quest to save the universe with his quirky yet well-meaning assistant (pot plant), arrives on an infamous planet:
Castlewellan.
Home to the master-criminal known only as the Rampion, the planet is a lonely stronghold, with gravity so strong there is no hope of escape. Will the Rampion redeem himself, and atone for his past actions by aiding our travellers? Can he overcome the deep-seated grudge he holds against the Horticulturalist?

"I thought I'd get that done on the way here," said Hort. "I hope you don't mind."

She should have been standing on rock. After that scrolling introduction, she had expected nothing less than a forbidding, impenetrable fortress before her, stretching up to a black sky, where storm clouds loured. But the sky was pale yellow, and thick, tangible. Penelope put her hand up and felt the resistance of this creamy air; it parted around her skin and left ribbons of red smoke behind, curling and swirling from her fingers, and then dissipating.

"There's a grudge?" she said.

"More of a disagreement. I'll soon clear it up. This is lovely, isn't it?"

They were on a beach of pale blue sand, with a still lake ahead, and the atmosphere of early morning about it. It was beautiful, but far too reminiscent of Earth, as it had been on postcards and with inspirational slogans and yet never quite as she had seen it in person.

She looked down at her own body, expecting to see, what? An improvement, because of the setting? In this beautiful place, surely she should be the best version of herself? But no. There were the low lumps of her breasts, the curve of her stomach. She was still in the same clothes. Her stomach hurt, and she wasn't even real any more, and she didn't have a stomach.

"Outwards, not in," Hort reminded her gently, and she looked into his young, open face and returned his smile. He held out a hand to her, and she took it, and allowed herself to be twirled around on the sand, leaving corkscrews of red smoke behind her.

"This way."

He steered her to the edge of the lake, and then into it, and yet they made no splash because it was not wet. Dry water. It had a thicker texture again, in a darker blue than the sand, and was opaque; Penelope couldn't see her feet. But it was not difficult to wade through. Hort led her further out. Up to her knees. Then her waist.

"Are we going to swim for it?" she asked. She had never been a strong swimmer.

"Not exactly. Come on."

"Is the prison on the lake? Is it an island?"

"I thought I explained that. The planet is the prison. Why make a building or delineate an area? Instead, simply select a planet. There are so very many to choose from, Pea. You have no idea. Castlewellan fits the bill nicely. It's flexible enough that Rampion can spread out, and be happy."

"Happy?"

Hort kept wading; Penelope felt the dry water lap her chest, then slide up to her neck. It had a delicate smell, now it was nearly up to her nose, that reminded her a little of garlic.

"Of course! Nobody wants him to attempt to leave. It's in everyone's interests to keep him in a pleasant mood. Right, relax. Pretend to breathe normally."

"Everyone?"

"You know. The powers that be."

"I don't know, though."

"Oh yes, that's right. You don't," he said.

"Did *you* know," she said, on the cusp of submersion, aware of the trembling edge of fear in her voice, "that Castlewellan is a thick conifer? It makes an effective screening hedge. And Rampion is a spiked flower. It's also known as the Rapunzel plant."

"I love it when you talk about classifications," he told her, and then the dark blue substance was up to her mouth, over her nose; her eyes were under the surface, and everything was different again.

The colour was gone.

Underneath, everything was clear and fresh, like Earth air, and she could see for miles – much further than her slight short-sightedness would usually allow.

There was nothing to see with her new, miraculously sharp vision. This was an empty place, without life, without forms.

"Look down," said Hort. Lazy swirls of red ejected from his mouth and spiralled, downwards this time. She watched them descend into gradations of darkness, down to a blue she would have described as navy. The dry lake was so very deep. They had not been walking on a surface at all, had they? Had she imagined the feeling of the ground beneath her feet? Where had the sand gone?

She realised they were sinking, just like the spirals. From one anxiety to another: deep water, and the dark. This was a collection of experiences she didn't like wrapped up in a picturesque bow.

"Breathe," Hort reminded her. The word created an instinctive reaction. She breathed in, then out, and although she could feel her lungs filling with the weight of the substance that was not quite water, she found it was not very unpleasant, as a sensation. It resembled being full up after a large meal: pressure, with a hint of heartburn.

Her eyes began to pick out constructions below, towers of sticks, or maybe metal rods. Pylons. As she focused, her improved sight meant she could make out slim wires between each uppermost point. And then slow-moving boxes, travelling along the wires, all moving in the same direction, further down, into the gloom.

Cable cars.

"There's one coming along shortly," said Hort. He pointed, and she saw it. A wooden car with a sliding door would be passing directly underneath them shortly. It would, in fact, be perfect timing.

She opened her mouth to speak, then shut it again.

"It's fine," Hort reassured her.

"It appeared," she said. Her voice sounded normal. Red smoke slipped from between her lips. "It wasn't there before."

"It means he knows we're here. It's a good sign. He's happy to talk to us. Keep sinking and we'll hop in once we reach it."

A cable car, neat and old-fashioned: it reminded her of a holiday she once took to Garda, in Italy, when she was first married. Graham had been keen to go, to be involved in the business of finding flowers at first, and they had justified the holiday on that grounds. *What's this one?* he would say, *Have you got it already?* as they wandered the Dolomites, driving the hired car up roads that petered out into tracks, and then stopped altogether. Reversing back round twenty hairpins to return to the town for an evening meal; Malcesine, that was the name of the place. And the mountain directly above it was Monte Baldo, linked directly to the town via the wires of the cable car network that took tourists up and down all day.

Standing in the car in their walking boots, holding fleeces and protective gear (a rucksack with Thermos flask, penknife, and torch, she remembered – did they never travel light?), she remembered how they smiled at each other. It had been a silent joke at the expense of the other passengers, mainly couples, some with young families, dressed in summer shorts and dresses – one woman had been wearing a bikini top, for heaven's sake. As the car rose they began to shiver, and when they stepped out at the peak to find a smattering of snow there had been a general grumbling and heading straight for the glass-walled cafe for hot drinks. How ill-prepared people could be.

She looked at her own clothes. Her skirt, her shoes, her cardigan. No supplies, no backpack. Was she the worst kind of tourist now?

"Here it comes," he said, but it turned out to be a leisurely business, to grab the thick wooden handle as the car passed, slide back the door, and walk inside. It was a relief to put her feet on a floor, even if it wasn't really a floor and if she had seen what it really was her mind would have been blown.

Blow:

gust flurry puff breeze tempest typhoon bash biff crack cut shock slam slap slug jolt misfortune tragedy gasp heave wallop

Her vision trembled, threatened to fracture.

Don't, she told herself. *Outwards, not in.*

She focused on the long slatted bench running down the side of the car opposite the door, and the words began to recede. She took a seat. Hort remained standing, looking out of the window to her left. He had a pleasing profile, so she concentrated on that as the downwards trajectory made her stomach tighten.

"Are we on the way to see him? The Rampion?"

"Sort of," said Hort. "He's everywhere, really. The run is his thought process, and the car is his consciousness. Soon we'll start getting a view of what he's thinking about right now. His roots are way down there, inserted into the core of the planet. This blue stuff is his food."

Food:

liquid air water atmosphere sunlight sky

She forced herself to concentrate. "Roots. The Rampion is actually a plant."

"Some of the best people are."

"He's a plant," she repeated.

"Why are you saying it like that?" Hort frowned at her.

"I'm sorry, I just… So this is growth? He grows this cable car?"

"You see a cable car? That's delightful! Yes, he grows it. Isn't it amazing? I've always wanted to see it. It's a most singular form of garden."

Garden:

collection memory assortment explanation reason justification personality

On and on went the words. She put her hands over her ears knowing it would make no difference and the sounds and meanings were inside her. Reality began to break apart. Hort turned green, then his face slowed and elongated, as if he was being viewed on an old television screen in an area with bad reception. She recoiled from him, felt the hard wooden wall of the cable car against her back, reached behind to press her hands against it. It was solid, her hands could feel it: she was intact. Penelope, on a journey. She breathed. She breathed.

"Can you keep it together?" said Hort. "That's it. Well done. Well done."

It all reasserted itself into Castlewellan: a cable car, a bench, and a view. The atmosphere had turned darker. She moved her hand in front of her face; the curling trails it left were black.

"You're getting the hang of it," he said. "What strength of will you have! I love it! This might work. It might actually work."

"What might work?"

"No questions! Out, not in! Come, look out of the window and see a wonderful mind at work! It's a treat of a lifetime."

She stood, joined him at the window, and focused with her new eagle-worthy eyesight upon a scene of intricacy, detail, and such breadth that she couldn't, at first, make sense of it.

Buds.

White, unopened, reproductive flower buds, with heavy black seams and outlines. They moved; they swayed in the sea, a huge amount of them, spaced at regular intervals but all with tiny individualistic details, differences in size and shape.

What kind of flower would emerge? She didn't recognise it, and found she didn't care for it: this spread of one kind of plant alone. There was no variation, no diversity here.

"I don't know this genus."

"They are memory. Thought. Experience. They are whatever he wants them to be."

The cable car sped onwards on its soft decline, into further darkening territory. The buds started to appear closer to the window. Penelope could see fine wires, or perhaps hairs, that grew from the unattached peduncles, stretching out to join to others. A flash of blue light shot along the path of one such hair to reach a bud that opened into a corolla of vibrant white petals, glowing, pulling far back from the central disc.

It resembled a sunflower, she thought; not only for the separation and configuration of the petals, but in the way it moved, swinging its head around to follow the path of the cable car as it if was the sun, albeit at a ferocious speed.

In the disc was a face.

It was human, male and old. It looked very like an actor Penelope liked from an old prison drama about hope and perseverance. Morgan Freeman, that was his name.

Morgan Freeman smiled at her.

She was beginning to get used to these tricks. It was a way for her consciousness to make sense of whatever was actually upon the flower, and keep it bearable for her, of course. She doubted that a giant alien criminal plant being did actually look like Morgan Freeman.

More flashes of light through the hairs leading from that flower, and more opening buds, every one containing a Freeman.

"Greetings!" said Hort. "You know who I am?"

The Freemans smiled wider.

"So you're ready for my visit, then? You're not angry? That's good. I really am sorry about what happened. Let's move right along. Let's talk about Tearthumb, and the Timetape heist. You used the tape to send an unregistered package to Earth."

Earth:

home soil meaning planet base ground reason

"No," said Penelope, faintly.

The Freeman heads, still blooming, looked interested in this, but also faintly puzzled. There was that benign humorous expression she recognised from his occasional comic roles.

"You didn't send that package?" Hort pressed.

Personally? Of course not. Nothing is done personally.

The voice was inside her head, but she also strongly felt the suggestion of a new presence behind her. She turned, at the same time as Hort, to find a constantly shifting set of physical characteristics in the cable car. It was a flickering outline of a person – two arms, two legs, a head – that changed from masculine to feminine, small to big, short to tall, showing every deviation for only an eyeblink before it shifted onwards, each piece changing independently, like a police photofit.

"The Rampion," said Hort. There was wonder in the way he said the name. "I'm honoured."

Horticulturalist. For this, we are here. Tearthumb. Things were taken. Things were given. Aren't they? What will you take from this place?

The mouth of the flickering outline did not move. The voice sounded inside her, and it was not exactly like hearing somebody speak. It resembled the act of recalling a conversation that had happened earlier, somehow – for both the Rampion's voice and her own, with no guarantee exactly those words had been used. It was a slippery business.

"Will you give me the answers I want?"

I give what I choose to give. You know this. I have my own reasons. You may owe me, if you wish.

"I just thought I'd check if you were willing to help me out," said Hort. He was smiling, but the line of his mouth was tight, far from his usual grin.

You wondered if I might change, come the end? No, I will remain the same.

Hort took the cardboard box from his sleeve. He turned it upside down and a steady stream of black dust began to pour from it, forming a pyramid on the cable car floor. "Does this change anything?"

The figure flickered through combinations.

That is from – a long pause, and then Penelope's brain filled in – **Calendula.**

"It is," said Hort. "It is, forgive me for saying so, your mother, is it not? Her remains."

You spoke to her?

"I did. A while ago. I never thought I would stand in your presence and tell you this. In fact, I find I'm glad to have the opportunity to do so. She spoke lovingly of you. She asked me to leave you alone."

A silence followed. The blue darkened a shade more. It was getting difficult to see.

"I've always thought of calendulas as vivid opportunists," said Penelope, uncomfortably. "Fast growers."

I am glad, too. I have long desired to tell you things.

The figure raised an ever-changing arm and pointed back to the window. She turned, looked out over the thousands of buds, glaring white. The strands of hair that linked them had surged into bright electrical life, pulsating: the Morgan Freeman flowers were dying, their petals dropping away, sinking. A host of new buds were opening, and inside each one was the same image upon the central disc – a replicated scene, in miniature.

Penelope fixed her attention on just one, concentrated upon it, and found she could zoom in as if looking through a telescope; the edges of her vision turned black, but no part of the central scene evaded her. She felt she could have seen down to its very atoms.

The bud no longer seemed botanical. It was more like one facet of the compound eye of an insect, each part reflecting the same whole. And the image it showed was a soft orange swatch of material, speckled with white dust – perhaps chalk. The cloth scrunched itself into a ball then unwound to lie unwrinkled. The chalk dust did not shift. The cloth repeated the action, and as Penelope watched she felt a prickling awareness that it was not a cloth at all. It was space. It was the universe and the stars within it in rapid flux, folding and turning and squirming while the fixed star dust gave the illusion of solidity.

Deeper in, with her forensic vision. One speck from the scattering of dust enlarged to become a solid yellow planet, dense and real and entirely there. Zooming in further still yellow filled her vision, and then broke apart to form squirming life: repulsive, maggotish.

See? Such possibility.

Could it be a soup of creation? From random blind writhing an order began to erupt in a way that was deeply familiar to her. Plants. Their genesis, speeded up, was textbook: shoots emerging, pushing up, while roots pushed down. Energy converting to enzymes, sending out one message. Grow. The splitting and emerging of a leaf, then two. Long, slim buds emerged. Was it – Lilium longiflorum? Her heart was alive with pain and promise. But no, no, these were no flowers she knew. Asymmetrical, multicoloured, delicate: she felt a maternal rush, anyway, for the sheer fragile ridiculousness of their creation.

It ended in death, of course. The death of each plant hurt her as she watched, even though two more would replace it and cover the planet. A pinprick of a hole was left by each tiny absence. Or perhaps that was her imagination? She could not tell where her perception and the presentation differed.

Each generation of living flowers grew tall on the fertilizer provided by the remains of the generation before, and then a subtle change took place; at the end of each growth cycle the disc developed a fuzzy greyish substance that rose up, rather like the downy fluff created by the Slender Bulrush. Was there an updraft of hot air from the soil of the planet? Up and up they climbed, lingering for longer each time before beginning to fall once more.

Another change: the fluff began to stick together, clinging to each other, apparently buoyed by the contact, rotating in the sky to form chains of life that then sprouted anew. The growths spread out sideways to form platforms, stabilising their positions. These joined to create a levels, reaching so high that the yellow tinge of the planet turned grey, and then black. The plants had left their ancestors far, far below. They were surviving off-planet. Somehow, they had found a way to continue to live as they explored beyond their environment.

The growth continued, interweaving to reach an apex. It had created a pyramid. Penelope refocused to the tip of the structure. Time stopped. All development was frozen.

A seed, one tiny seed, was fired from the pyramid into space. Time accelerated once more, or perhaps the seed really was travelling at an incredible pace, so fast that she had to readjust her vision, zoom out, zoom out, until the seed broke free of the cloth itself. A release. An escape. An audacious, amazing act.

My birth.

But what was beyond the cloth? That small square of material? She zoomed out further and further; how far could she see into what lay around the universe itself?

Enough.

The buds turned grey, and died. Light failed. The deep blue darkness in which they were standing, floating, being, was a comforting sadness. Nothing made sense.

"You travelled beyond," said Hort.

I did. I wanted knowledge.

"You dealt with the…?" Hort's mouth was moving, but no sound came out. Penelope reached for an understanding of this new concept in her own language. It was as if she was climbing a mountain to reach a vantage point so high, so extreme, that one had to then wait for clouds to clear just enough to allow one beam of sunlight to cut through and illuminate, at an oblique angle, one sliver of the land below.

"Armillaria?"

Armillaria. Not a plant. A genus of fungus. Penelope searched her memory. Armillaria solidipes, a honey fungus, was the largest living thing on Earth, spreading through trees in a forest in Oregon to measure miles across. It was not her field of expertise, but a fascinating area nonetheless.

I did. It told me what I wanted to know, in exchange for a task. A delivery.

"Ahhhhh," breathed out Hort, leaning forward. "That explains it. That explains it. Now I see. The Vice. The Armillaria gave it to you, to have it taken to Earth. It's out-of-universe technology."

You have your answer.

"Why Earth?" said Penelope.

You wish to know. But why should I wish to tell you?

"I don't know."

The constantly changing head tiled, as if thought was taking place. Then the Rampion's voice, in her head, said:

I find I have changed, come the end. How unexpected. I will give you a gift, pet of the Landscaper.

"What did you call me?"

Look out of the window. I will give you my life.

"We should get going, actually," said Hort. "We don't have enough time."

We have enough.

She looked out, aware that Hort might choose to make a doorway and whisk her away at any moment. Was there time for more answers? She would take what she could get. The electrical flashes were already firing, and all of the buds were opening, all of them. This time the pearls within the discs were not the same. Each one was different; each one was an event, a happening, a moment from a life, seen through the eyes of the one who had lived it – the Rampion.

Penelope focused on one, then another, then another, randomly, taking in as many as she could. There was no separation between herself and the Rampion; she relived each pearl memory with him. It was an opportunity to truly understand another being, to make sense of this alien universe that had, so far, proved impenetrable to her. She zoomed in, and in, and lost herself within him:

THE RAMPION REMEMBERS

My mother puts her thorns to my roots and cuts, cuts, and there is pain. With that sharp arrival comes the fear of disconnection, of a future without her, but my mother blossoms over me and lets me smell her sweet scent of surety: *You are the culmination. You will be unbound.*
She cuts away all and then sticks four of the nubs into her heart-dirt to replenish me. This is the food of seedlings and I guzzle it, knowing it is my last taste of Calendula. Once my wounds heal I will be fired out into the unknown, where I will freeze until I find the elements of life once more: air, warmth, light, liquid. I am terrified. What is that sound? I am screaming, of course, I am screaming. I scream for my mother, but I am the culmination. I will find the answers she wants and return them to her. She needs to know

why we exist, I tell the first creature I meet on some sun-circling planet, where I have awoken and plunged my roots into its depths. It is a travelling facility, a way-point for non-photosynthetic beings that use machines to make their journeys, spending so much of their finite little lives this way. There is an order to the universe I had not expected to find, and so many kinds of creature with so many languages to learn, but not one of them has the answers I seek.

Still, this one is amazed at how I can freeze, revive and reseed, floating where I will through space and emerging from that stasis to grow large once more in the right conditions. It seems particularly taken with the part where I cut my own roots to make limbs, enabling locomotion in a fashion it understands.

I like its enthusiasm. So when it tells me through a translation mechanism that it, too, wants answers and has plans to find them, I am intrigued. I did not realise lower life forms had such thoughts. Or perhaps the translation is awry.

It asks me if I could be useful.

Is this really a word that applies to me? I am new at such concepts, but this one sounds like it might bring me further to my aim, so I say

YES.

I am trembling.

My new-growth leaves will not stop shaking.

Ridiculous. I am the Rampion. I have built a fearsome reputation throughout the universe and built a vast, stretching network of thieves, liars and utilisers.

But all my actions have been for this moment in the presence of an Armillaria, when it considers my proposition and says it will agree to it.

It will tell me why there is life. Any life. My life.

I am close to the dwarf planet of Alchemilla Mollis, having completed countless acts to track down this one small hole that leads to the sea between all universes. I have made so many bargains to reach this point. And now there is only one more trade to make, before it will tell me what I need to know. I must deliver one solid item, instantly, secretly, to a planet of no importance, and then return it once a certain task is done. The Armillaria I am trading with calls it:

Ear

th.

This will require Timetape. No other method can transport the object it is giving me at such speed. The object has a surprising weight to it.

We conclude our business. It will give me my answer when the task is completed. I depart quickly. It's better not to look too hard at this place, this form of existence. I wish to keep my own reality

intact roots once more, how strange, so long after those first cuts by my mother. I have grown into my own captivity, stretching down into the core. I am shackled to it, this place, this warm substance in which I float that keeps me docile somehow, unwilling to seed. Is it a soporific? I feel the desire to return to my original form. The end should resemble the beginning, should it not? Circles. They have planted me. My roots are stuck deep to the centre of this planet and I cannot cut myself free.

How is this done?

I have come so close to an answer to the greatest question, and yet the one piece of knowledge I need right now eludes me.

Maybe it is simpler than I think, and the answer lies within me. Maybe I am tired of travelling, and so I am letting myself be still.

All this time, and I still do not know what I really think and feel.

So I will be here, on Castlewellan. I will put my energies into my own budding and I will turn this world into a garden of my mind. How big can I become? How far can I

grow under the floor and emerge in a chamber, beyond the traps and sensors, to retrieve the ring. That is the plan, and so I begin. I grow. My newfound non-photosynthetic friends urge me on, and I find I wish to impress them. Also, I do not seem to have the same interest in concepts of ownership as they have, so I have told them I will take no share in the treasure, which has pleased them greatly.

Instead, you will owe me, I tell them.

Owing is very much more understandable to me than

owning. Who can possibly own what? For how long? Maybe it is an attempt to pretend that death is not the only pure concept in this universe. If one truly and incontrovertibly possesses something then one cannot die. This is, perhaps, what children are an attempt to do in non-chloro terms. They are the ultimate attempt at possession.

I die all the time. My leaves wither and new growth arrives. I am not a permanence. I am on a sliding scale of potential. I grow.

The chamber where the ring is kept is above my farthest tendril. I slide a shoot up to the barred window and anchor myself in place. Then I sprout anew and make my way over to the cushion where the ring rests.

I slide inside the ring and create a tiny coronet of leaves so it is wrapped within me, before starting to retreat. Meanwhile, my cut roots sit with my friends, who whisper - *that's it, Ramp. You've got it. Now bring it back here. Bring it*

back to Tearthumb. I have a contact there.

Dandelion is amazed. I know her well enough to read her emotions. We have completed so many tasks together. Our wills have often aligned.

On Tearthumb itself? That's impossible.

You think because they are religious zealots that they cannot be bribed? I say the opposite. Religion is the ultimate bribe, is it not? Believers do good things for a high price, and a fabulous eternal reward. So they are already used to such terms.

Dandelion is from Monotropsis Odarata. This means her real body is in storage and she travels only as a consciousness that takes over the nearest creature of flesh upon arrival on a new planet, overriding any existing personality. She has done this many times, meaning that she is well travelled, reliable, and less concerned about certain moral issues than other beings. I trust her with this task.

Make contact. Pick up the Timetape.

What then? she asks.

Our meeting is taking place on a marsh planet. She is within an amphibious form; she keeps jutting out a long tongue, using it to lave her greasy face. I can tell she does not like this automatic reaction. Who would? I dare say the amphibian didn't care for it either.

Then you find somebody. To make a collection. You wait until the collecting is done, and then you return. To me. And, for this, I will owe you.

Dandelion looks around, in the wet darkness. Her tongue juts out, and this time she manages to control the action and put it back in her mouth without licking herself. I snake out a growth and tickle her under her bulbous chin, just to feel her skin. It is dry, even though it looks slimy. What an uncomfortable way to exist. What a ridiculous creation, with no discernible point. She flinches; she is ticklish. Is that the reaction of the body, or of the consciousness inside?

Think of your task as planting a seed. There is a goal that needs to be

placed a sleeper seed of myself within the heart of the palace, and it will only awake from its dormancy upon my command. It will grow and bloom, and emit a sweet, cloying scent that will send the guards of the Ghost Orchid to sleep. Then you can take off your disguise, step inside, and claim him as your

—⟲

own way of approaching these problems, and interfering directly has long been uninteresting to me. The joy is in the manipulation, and I feel it now as I bribe the first, cajole the second, threaten the third.

The non-photosynthetics were good teachers, but I need them no longer. I understand enough of how they operate. Besides, my first crew are long dead in the way that only flesh creatures tied to one body can die – with a wordless permanence that suits their decision to stop growing.

They are afraid of me now. Or perhaps they are in awe of me because of how I am unbound by their rules, their drawbacks. There is nothing the Rampion cannot give or take. I've heard that in the vibrations of many planets. I am becoming a legend, yet the more I accomplish, the more tendrils I twine around this universe, the more I think of Mother.

I will return with my answer as soon as this last task is complete. It falls to Dandelion now.

There are lights in the distance. Crafts are approaching. Ahh, finally the non-photos come for me, thinking to exact their own form of justice, not realising that to apply their rules to me is a ridiculous

—⟲

1. *Violation of the Ghost Orchid, starting the Dendrophylax War.*
2. *The Powis Castle burglary, leading to an unauthorised use of the Wormwood Ring, directly causing the destruction of the Artemisian people.*
3. *The masterminding of the theft of Tearthumb Timetape, enabling unapproved transportation of solid matter.*
4. *Direct communication with an Armillaria.*

They have saved the largest offence till last. The representatives of the Sequoia do not even dare to look at me as I speak. They are afraid of me. Of what I know.

Therefore you will be fixed into the core of Castlewellan, a specially prepared high-density planet for the term of your natural life cycle.

I was expecting this, and yet it still affects me deeply. I hoped that I might be banished back to my home planet. I could have been happy there. I could have sworn never to leave. But word has reached me that the virus has taken the life from Calendula, and left it barren. Mother. Mother.

And my last answer, to the greatest of questions. Where is Dandelion? How can she find me?

Will I ask things of them? Will I beg? Will I promise to owe them anything, everything?

No. I will not. I am quiet, and I submit. It will not be long now, anyway, until The Virus comes for me too, and I get to meet the only being that wields a power as great as mine in this little universe. The green disease spreads through Castlewellan at a ferocious speed and I am dying, my memories are swallowed, reduced to unformed mush, but there is still time to tell my story, is there not? This is why I grew this garden. Yes, I will tell it.

Not to the Horticulturalist, though. I cannot thank him, even though he brings a final comfort in the form of the dust of my dead mother.

It was all for nothing. But then, does that not fit with my knowledge, and the one gap I leave behind?

Yes, this ending makes sense. And I race to open all my buds and show everything to a shadow of a fragment of a non-photosynthetic mind, who will barely comprehend what she sees. But still, I ask her to witness my garden, my memories, my life.

Remember me, little one. Take me in.

FLEEING **THE SCENE**

The buds oozing, dribbling down, the pearls lost, their shells breaking apart like cracked eggs to reveal vivid emerald yolks. The virus had arrived.

Penelope turned away from the window, unable to witness the destruction of such beauty. Hort was still, his hand to his mouth, tears in his eyes. The Avatar was gone. The dust that was all that remained of the Rampion's mother had scattered across the floor of the cable car and the wall behind was bulging inwards. In the centre of the bulge was a spreading patch of malevolent, glowing green.

"Hort," she said. "It's here. I can't—"

He reached for her, and she moved into his fierce hug. "I promise," he whispered, "I can save this. I know where we need to go next."

"But—"

"Shh." What good could it do, anyway, to point out that the Rampion was beyond saving? All of its memories, all of its knowledge, was being lost, destroyed. A hole appeared in the centre of the bulge and the wall of the cable car sizzled, as if the virus was an acid, dissolving all it touched. So much suffering, so much loss.

"Come," said Hort. He traced a rectangle with one finger, and the white doorway began to peel back. "Let's travel."

Travel:

move journey abandon embrace

The word would not be still and she was too full of fear, of misery, to hold back the echoing ramifications as it multiplied inside her, making the raucous chirruping of the just born as it splintered into meaning

after meaning

after meaning

Then – silence.

Cold.

A deep, white iciness, leaving her brittle. Everything had disappeared, including Hort, and the cable car, and the Rampion.

A deep roar rumbled underneath her.

Penelope looked down to find herself suspended over a vast black pit. The roar came again, and for a moment she was bathed in the hot breath of it. It came to her that these were the death throes of the Rampion, incomprehensible in size and scope. The black was not one space, but a dwelling of many rooms and caves and tunnels that made up one creature. If she was to fall into it she would be lost.

She did not move. She was suspended, and as she looked at her own body – so familiar, so beautifully ugly normal – Penelope realised she was also a dwelling. Her breasts fell apart and swung outwards, and she looked inside her own chest at the place where she lived.

It was less impressive than the Rampion, definitely. There were not so many rooms, but still it was a neat little cottage that contained the things she labelled as part of herself. There was the ordered bookshelf of her botanical knowledge, and there was the rug of her childhood. There was the sofa of her comfort zone next to the side table of her marriage, and upon the table, in a silver vase, sat one Lily. It was not the largest object in the living room, but it was by far the most beautiful. She stared at it.

Lily.

But the room was cold, her chest was cold. She shivered. Could she start a fire? There was a range cooker in the kitchen, burning brightly. Too brightly. Its door was open, and the fire had a strong pull to it. The objects in the cottage were shaking, rattling, edging towards it.

"No," said Penelope. She wanted to grab the Lily, to keep it safe, but her hands were too big, too clumsy, to reach inside herself. She watched as smaller objects, as if under the spell of magnetism, flew to the range and disappeared inside to burn.

A small fish in a bowl.

A backpack.

"Take me in," said a deep, groaning voice, below her: the Rampion. "Here." Up, out of the pit, came a shooting star, so bright, fast and straight; she reached out as a reflex, and caught it. It was a small, hard object of burnished brown. She recognised it immediately as the seed of the Aesculus hippocastanum – a chestnut.

Take me in.

Penelope put the chestnut inside herself, on the fire. At first it seemed the flames would roast it and turn it to ash, but as she watched the chestnut began to grow. It took root in her hearth. A small, strong shoot erupted from the crown of the seed. It was starting the process of turning into a tree.

She closed her breasts back up, then folded her cardigan over them just as she felt an almighty shove between her shoulder blades and she fell

LILY, **IN BLOOM**

Lily: Right, it's on. You start.

Graham: No, you start.

Lily: You. I can't remember the words. You.

Graham: You can't remember the words? I sang it to you every night for years!

Lily: For the years you were there, until I was five and you split up with Mum, and you left. And then you only sang it on one weekend a month. It might have felt like a lot of singing to you, but to me it wasn't enough to really stick in the memory.

[Pause.]

Graham: Well now I don't want to sing it.

Lily: I'm just saying, you start and

it'll come back to me.

Graham: I wanted to be there.

Lily: It's not a criticism. I know it
was the best thing, for all
of us. Just don't– Don't
remember it as perfect. As more
than it was.

Graham: But I'm a parent. That's what
parents do.

Lily: Look, this was your idea.
Sing the bloody song.

Graham: No, it's okay. I can't really
remember it either. I made it up
in the first place. It was years
ago. A really long time ago.

Lily: It wasn't that long ago.

Graham: Do you want to turn that thing
off, then? Why did you want to
record it, anyway?

[Pause.]

Lily: It's such a shame that nobody
else has ever heard it. It seems
wrong to not leave a copy of it
behind. I thought it was a
proper song, you know, a
popular song, a–

Graham: A hit record.

Lily: Yes! A hit record. Top of the
Pops.

Graham: Known the whole world over. No.
           It was just made up. I haven't
           thought of it for years, but
           when we were in the basement,
           digging, the rhythm just came
           back to me, and then the words,
           all of them. It's so strange,
           how memory works.

[Pause.]

Lily: Do you think the swamp has
           dried out everywhere?
Graham: I don't know.
Lily: It's such a weird, spongy
           texture now. Maybe we should
           try eating it.
Graham: Now that sounds like a
           terrible idea.
Lily: At some point, it's going to
           become our only choice.
Graham: We still have tinned food left.
           How long has it been?
Lily: Nine days.
Graham: We'll be fine for a while yet.
           If the swamp dries to a point
           where we can walk on it, maybe
           we should go looking for help.
Lily: For now, though, we'll keep
           digging out the basement.

[Pause.]

Graham: What do you think you'll find down there?

Lily: A note. Maybe she left a note. On the table. Let's dig out the table.

[Pause.]

Graham: Okay, we'll dig out the table.

Lily: A note could have dropped to the floor. So if it's not there, we should also dig out the floor.

Graham: Okay. The floor.

Lily: It won't take long. It was fairly easy work today, wasn't it?

Graham: It was fine, sweetie.

Lily: Yeah.

[Pause.]

Lily: I'll just turn this off. It was a silly idea.

Graham: Wait.

[Cough.]

Graham: You might feel very little,

but you're growing every day,
and soon you'll overtake me,
in each and every way.
You're going to be amazing,
and everyone will see,
that you've got all the best
bits,
the very best of me.

HAVING A USE

I once read an article online – I can't remember where – about a woman who remembered everything. There was not a moment of her life, no matter how boring, how inconsequential, that she could not recall.

What's more, she could perform this feat by date and time. The interviewer asked her: *Where were you on the sixth of July 1998, at 6:23 p.m.?* She replied: *Microwaving dinner, at home. It was a ready-prepared Chicken Madras with pilau rice, sitting side by side in two black plastic compartments, and the smell was just beginning to drift through the kitchen. The radio was on. It was playing 'Vienna' by Ultravox, which is a song I'd heard fifty-two times before but I've always liked it so I turned it up a bit, and it had just reached the middle instrumental section as I fetched a knife and fork from the cutlery drawer.*

There are some memories we can happily label unimportant. I'm not sure that's the same thing as being happy to lose them, if we have to be aware of the loss.

Would it be easier to lose bad memories? I suspect it would have upset her deeply if she had been forced to reply: *I was taking a phone call from my father. He had pulled his car over to the hard shoulder of the motorway, on the way home from the hospital, because he couldn't stop crying. The initial tests had shown it had already reached his liver and they had sat him down and told him hours ago, and he had nodded, and said he understood. But in that minute, 6:23 p.m., it had hit him, and he had phoned to say that he couldn't see the road for crying, that it was dangerous, that he didn't know how he would get home. I told him to take his time, which was a stupid thing to say. I blushed, and wished I hadn't said it. That's all I thought, at that moment, and I will remember it forever.*

I can appreciate that it is good to let things go; I wouldn't mind letting that particular memory out of my head. But that memory belongs to me, and not to the woman who could remember everything. It's a memory that defines me. *Take your time*, when there is no time. I'll apologise for it in my head forever.

I just wish I could remember why a goldfish is important to me.

I know it is. Or was. I know it has something to do with my father. But the piece of me that recalls it has disappeared.

"I'm so sorry," says Hort, "I just couldn't collect you all up this time."

Although he looks the same as he did on Earth, I've never been more aware that I'm not seeing the real him at all. It never seemed to matter so much, before.

We are back at his Ingenious Storage Solution, and I'm in my familiar form again, which is also not the real me. Not any more. But at least I'm surrounded by Earth's fauna in the form of my Collection. They sprout within the vast space. Not all of them: that would be overwhelming.

Instead Hort has arranged, somehow, for only the examples of an English country garden to bloom: daffodils, hearts' ease, flox. Meadowsweet and lady smocks. There's a song that comes to mind. I don't understand how I could sing it right now, in its entirety, and yet not say whether I once owned a goldfish. There's a strange, sweet smell in the air. It's artificial, not floral, and it sits on the stinging curve of my nostrils. What is it? I don't know any more. I don't know. It's lost to me.

We are strolling, arm in arm, through this facsimile of a sweet summer day. I spy a rose: fimbriata.

"Look!" says Hort, pointing to it. "That's our flower. Remember?"

"Of course," I tell him.

"That's good," he says, and pats my hand as if I am damaged, as if I am to be humoured, and I think of my father again. Then I think of the Rampion, and the way he said *non-photosynthetic beings*, and I feel sick. I stop walking. I pull my arm free from his and use my inferior, piecemeal remains of a long-dead brain to attempt to think clearly.

"The virus. It showed up on Castlewellan. It killed the Rampion."

"It did. The universe is a little bit less than it was, yet again. But we're making progress, Pea! We're getting answers, and we can beat this thing, and—"

"The Rampion knew. It knew the virus was coming for it. It realised as soon as we arrived. It knew."

"Ah," says Hort. He nods.

"The virus follows you, doesn't it?"

"No, that's not it. That's not it."

"It's intelligent, and it's trying to stop you. It's moving with purpose."

He hesitates, then says, "It's very difficult to explain. It would be easier if I could just..." He lifts his hands to my head and I jerk back. Those wide green eyes flash me a look of surprise, pain. "I thought you trusted me."

"I do," I say, although that is not exactly the truth any more.

"Then let me give you your answers, okay? In the best way. For both of us."

He puts his fingers on my temples. Here comes the scrolling prologue, with the uplifting music. Here comes the story of Hort:

The Horticulturist:
A Tale of Destiny

Senescence: the goal of every civilization. To leave behind corporeal form and die back, as one creation, to a state of existence unfettered on a cellular level. Some do not know that is why they live, reproduce and then cease to be; others strive consciously, having evolved to the point of realisation that this physical universe does not have to constrain them, and that an existence awaits them, beyond.

The apex predator on the planet of Cynara senesced as one a long time ago, in a galaxy far, far away. All societal problems were solved as the Cynarans gave up their bodies to become beings of pure information. Not all survived the process: some lesser minds fragmented, fell apart, confusing consciousness with the wrapper in which it had been stored. These casualties were mourned, mourned deeply. But attachments to such concepts soon grew thin, and the Cynarans found death was no longer a deep concern to them.

This made it easier to accept the price they had to pay for their senescence. Their presence upon their home planet was no longer welcome. Rejection.

Plant matter could not survive contact with their new state of being. For no reason the Cynarans could divine, it soon began to dissolve, to melt, to turn into a mess of green sludge that swamped the planet. This led to the death of all animal matter, and the once beautiful and diverse planet became a barren rock.

Without a stimulating environment, the Cynarans suffered. They realised that the act of senescence was not a way to remove themselves from the world, but to better appreciate it. How ironic it was, then, that they were now the cause of its death.

But, existing in a state of pure information, they could travel where they wanted, and so -
onwards!
To Balera!
To Coniopteris!
To Eboracia!
To Nilssonia!

To Orontium!
To the next planet, and the next, and the next...
All dead, all dead. Soon after their arrival the
plant life turned a vivid green, and lost its cellular
structure, and any animal life perished in turn.
And so the Cynarans searched for an alternative,
and they found it.
A bubble.
A tiny hole in space/time, a flaw in the weaving
of the universe. A mark of a higher power,
perhaps? In their new state, this tiny anomaly
was a magnet. It drew their attention like a bright
object, far away, on a cold dark night.
They travelled to it and ventured inside it, and
found a different kind of existence, where there
was nothing that they could kill.
Time stopped, for them, and they were no longer
surrounded by death.
The bubble was malleable, and the Cynarans
found they could control it in their new forms,
shaping it to suit their needs. It was an ingenious
storage solution.
But it could not provide everything. It could not
assuage loneliness. So eventually the Cynarans,
finding themselves emptied of wants and desires
by the act of senescence, and no longer able to
find a provocation for further thought or action
through the presence of other life forms, decided
as one to put themselves into a state of torpor.
As one?
Not quite.

One of their number faked sleep, because he knew that his destiny lay on a different path. He was going to find a way to save plant life from his people, and therefore release the Cynarans back into the universe to share their higher insights with those who wanted to listen.
At first he practised alone, all the skills he would need for his mission.
He learned to transport himself across vast distances in moments. He learned to manipulate his own information to appear familiar to those who inhabited the planets he visited. Then, once he was ready, he set off: a tragic figure, knowing he would kill all he touched, racing against time to find places and creatures that could help him.
He had no name at first, but as planets started to die and the rumours started of a lone traveller who searched for gardens and collections of plant life, for experts who might know of a botanic that could survive his touch, he acquired a name:
The Horticulturalist.
His journey continues...

The scrolling words fade.

Hort and I are still standing in the English country garden; how can that be right? When I finally feel like I've travelled somewhere.

"You're a liar," I say. "Your very nature is m— m—" There's a specific word that suits this situation perfectly, but I can't remember it.

He bows his head. "Guilty as charged. In my defence, some of this stuff would be a lot to lay on a new relationship."

"You're the virus."

"I don't want to be! I'm looking for a solution. I'm actively engaged in trying to make myself a better person. That counts for something, right? I'm trying to save the universe here."

"From yourself."

"Yes." He crouches down and plucks a forget-me-not from a shy, peeping bush amidst the roses, then straightens up slowly. He can't meet my eyes. I think he's afraid of my admonishment. But I have to get this straight. I have to understand it.

"If you didn't go anywhere," I say, "then the universe wouldn't need saving."

"So you think I should just stay put, like the rest of my kind? Submit to endless sleep, and miss the chance to help others to senesce? You think I should stay cooped up in this box forever? I'm sorry Pea, I can't do that."

"Why not?"

He shrugs. "If you don't understand, that's fine. I'd love to have your approval, but I'm not beholden to it."

So. Nothing I can ever say will alter his behaviour. We are not equals. How could we be? I am completely dependant upon him. I am an idiot. I have been an idiot. I should have chosen to die with my daughter.

Hort is looking at me with such sympathy. How does he manage to be so human? Of course, it's me, projecting humanity upon him. No wonder his camouflage is so convincing. "We can still save the Earth," he says, softly. "That's why you agreed to come along. You remember that, right?"

"Save it from yourself."

"Just save it. Isn't that what's important now?"

Lily, I cling to you. Never let me forget you, Lily.

He fills up my silence with words. "I'm come so far on this journey, Pea. I'm sure you can see that I can't stop now. And my intentions, even if they were misguided to begin with, my intentions have always been good. We're so close, can't you feel it? As soon as I met you, I knew I was nearly there. The Vice, the Vice exists. It does something amazing, something I don't understand. Look what it did to your flowers. Here we stand, amidst plants that don't die in my presence. This is progress, Pea. I've never been so close to an answer as I am right now, and it's because of you, you're my lucky charm, my guiding star—"

"Stop," I tell him. "Stop."

"No, no, I can't, there's only one more place to go. Finally, I know the location of an Armillaria. I can ask it directly to give me the secret of the Vice." He takes my hand, and pats it. "Perhaps it's better if I just get cracking. I can see you don't agree with me, and that's fine. I promise, that's fine. But I have to do this, and maybe if you get some space to think about it you'll see why."

"Will you kill it? Will your presence kill this Armillaria?"

"I don't expect so," he says, as if the thought hadn't occurred to him. "Anyway, listen, I think you should stay put for this one. You're practically falling apart. Stay here. Rest." He glances around the garden and the flowers shrink away, to be replaced by that single bed, with grey emptiness beyond the glass walls, and a far-stretching steeple high above. It strikes me that this is really a cross between a church and a hospital, in its barest form. I am meant to both repent and convalesce here, conveniently, in time for Hort's return.

"No, I think I should come with you," I hear myself say.

"And risk another incident? You keep breaking into bits and I can't always gather all of you back in. Stay here. I'll be back soon. Settle in properly. This is your home now. It's your safe place."

"No, I don't think—"

He draws a rectangle with his finger, and steps through, and he is gone.

> • <

I sleep. I wake.

He does not return.

I sleep. I wake.

He does not return.

I realise I'm not really sleeping or waking.

The ipomea, known as Morning Glory, is a blazing purple trumpet flower, bearing five stripes that lead inwards to a soft white heart. It opens and closes with the sun; it is an automatic gesture. I've been behaving in the same way, thinking I'm still a creature of Earth, in the thrall of the sun and moon, taking part in their rhythms.

I give up sleeping.

It doesn't hurt.

He does not return.

I sleep. I sleep and sleep and sleep, to block out time, to escape the thought that I will never leave this place, not even in death, because I am already dead. Maybe I will lose more and more of myself in these episodes of instability I have, until I have degraded to the point of unusability. But I have a suspicion that will not be the same thing as death.

So I stay awake, and I think.

I've lost parts of myself. I have a seed inside me. I feel different.

Time is not passing. That means Earth is frozen, has been unchanged, for as long as I've been here. So Hort might not be lying about that. There's a possibility that Earth is still salvageable.

That doesn't change the feeling I have that time is passing for me. It is illusory, but still I'm travelling in the familiar forward motion of seconds, minutes, hours.

How long has passed?

How long might pass before Hort returns?

He might not return at all.

I decide to lose track of time, but this is not so easy to abandon as sleeping and waking. I can't escape the sensation of it passing me by, even if I'm not monitoring the amount.

Single bed, empty room. Grey sky that is not sky, beyond.

The Rampion's memories are fresh within me. They mingle with my own, and leave strange holes between.

I suspect one of us once had a goldfish.

Lonely
  solitary desolate isolated reclusive forsaken forgotten uncherished antisocial abandoned disconsolate empty
  old
  ancient inactive worn frayed tired fossilised mature decrepit seasoned senile grizzled hoary
  woman
  matron mother girl spouse female sow cow doe queen princess whore witch breeder

❯ • ❮

I can't find myself in words any more.

When Lily was little she would say, *I just want to understand*. That's part of my memory that remains, and I want to believe that I can keep it safe through the act of repetition. I think of Lily saying it, with her eyes and cheeks scrunched together like fresh, unfolding apple blossom. I think of it, think of it, think of it.

The unchanging grey outside the glass walls is unbearable. What I wouldn't give to see a Lilium longiflorum.

There was a War. I remember that too. It was not, looking at it from a fresh perspective, a big or important war. It was a small event that lasted for a blip of time, only affecting one planet. Not even all of that planet. The plants and nearly all of the animals weren't even aware it was taking place.

This war had seemed like a huge event because it had eaten away at the human notion of a shared history, which just goes to show what a ridiculous and downright lucky group of creatures humans are. They had a moment when they thought there could be such a thing as a collective agreement about the past, present and future. In fact, they thought that was how things were supposed to be.

Lily had just begun to walk when I first took her to nursery, so I could start to reclaim some time as my own, for my Collection. But I couldn't bear, at first, to leave the building. I couldn't escape the thought that she would know the difference between me being in the next room or a twenty-minute drive away, even though both were simply out of sight for her. I spent three weeks sitting in the reception area, straining to hear her laugh or cry, before the woman in charge kindly told me no more, go home. She's fine.

There was a bookshelf of old hardbacks next to the potted anthurium – a red fanned flower wrapped around a squashy yellow pistil – and I often took down a book of quotes from an old actor and raconteur; his name deserts me. There was a picture of his avuncular face on the cover and it appealed to me. I found myself thinking about one quote, between the anecdotes, often. It was—

Most of us are generally united by our doubts and divided by our convictions.

I think I liked it at the time because it suggested our vulnerabilities are what should bring us together, as humans, as a species. But now I'm ready to accept that nobody, anywhere, knows anything for sure and it's better that way. Doubt is a strength, not a weakness.

I wonder if I can't recall the name of that old celebrity because it's one of the pieces of me that floated away, the last time I lost myself. What a specific scrap of information to lose: the name of a person I never met, about whom I've formed assumptions based on a public persona purely because I felt he expressed a concept better than I could myself. That was enough to assume a connection, another long strand, a tenuous tendril.

I think about that for a long time.

Then, when I've finished thinking about it, I look back and realise no time has passed at all. It has telescoped up, folded within itself.

He does not return.

He may not return at all.

I really wish I could see a Lilium longiflorum again:

creamy curved petals, large, bold, not a delicate flower. It cannot be shaken apart, unlike a snowdrop. It is strident in its beauty.

Hort could make one appear simply by thinking of it. How did he do that? By commandeering my Collection, and placing it on his shelves. He said that any item on the shelves could be brought to form in this room.

I think of the lily.

I wish it to appear.

But that's not right: it's no longer a lily. It's a compression of information via the Vice.

I think of the disc that held the lily.

Of course, that's only a disc. It's a surface on which the information sits, rests, pretends to be still. The disc is like a layer of skin; it allows for the illusion that the entirety of one creation can be gathered in one place. I'm beginning to understand how silly that is. Even humans keep growing, although we can't see it at the moment of it taking place.

A very specific word pops into my head, and I find myself crying with gratitude for the gift of it.

Thigmomorphogenesis: the response of plants to stimulus. Pisum sativum – the pea, aptly enough – will grow tendrils to pull itself to different places when it senses touch, rainfall, wind, an insect walking upon it. I am the same. I am sprouting in so many directions, having been touched by so many things.

The Rampion's mind was a field of buds, ready to bloom upon command, and they were all interlinked by tendrils, too. Or were they electrical wires? Veins? Whatever they were, they deepened the connections, and made fresh ones.

I think of the words that belong around my Lilium

longiflorum, and all the connections it makes for me. I won't be afraid of this. I won't be scared of breaking apart.

I think of the way the lily grows on the Ryukyu Islands in Japan, and the way it's so toxic to cats, and the way it looked in the vase on the windowsill of my hospital bed after having my daughter, and I make a web of these things, and so many more things, until I feel full to bursting with them all.

Here it comes.

It grows straight out of the floor and then blooms, and it is perfect, just as I remembered. Tall, sturdy, intense in scent: it is real.

I lie down beside it, so I can look up at the underside of the petals, where the path of the veins turns a deeper shade, with a pink tinge. It's just like the soft lobes of my baby's ear. I concentrate, and make a field of the lilies, their heads raised above my own; they are a crowd of associations that take me back to myself better than any memory, separated from its time and place, could ever manage.

I don't need to be afraid of losing myself.

There is no myself.

Every part of me extends, touches, grows in and out, and spreads further still. Perhaps this is the start of understanding the universe.

> • <

This is the perfect time to grow all my favourite flowers, with the best connections to happy times, homes, holidays, walks in the sun, walks in the rain, garden after garden after garden. Their familiar names warm me: buttercup and heartsease and viola and marigold. I grow flowers so rare that my hands trembled as I held their seeds: lady slipper, middlemist, youtan poluo, the black bat.

How could I ever tire of this? The Collection will be all I need forevermore, so strong is my delight.

Then, slowly, slowly, the rapture fades.

Flowers cannot give me everything I need. The ones I pressed through the Vice number in their thousands, but they are all the same thing, in essence. They don't deliver experience. They can't fill all the gaps inside me.

I push the feeling down, but it will not go away. I want to be away from this place. To be elsewhere. Not the one who waits, but the one who sees new things, has new thoughts triggered, new blossoms of imagination. To collect, to grow, to own, to learn.

I have a better understanding of Hort now. When he told me what he is, I thought, *you should stop travelling.* I didn't really understand what I was asking of him. No wonder the other Cynarans chose to sleep.

That does not mean that I have forgiven him. My forgiveness is entirely irrelevant, anyway. Acts of genocide pale into comparison beside his efforts.

Stalin comes to mind – something he once said. I can't remember what.

I wonder where the Cynarans rest in their place. Do they have rooms like this one, glass and plain, with the option of a single bed? Or do they float together in a cloud, or a bath of liquid? I have no idea what they look like. Has Hort created a special environment for them? I'm guessing they need nothing, being creatures of pure information.

But Hort. Hort likes spaces and places and designs. The glass steeple above me is a testament to that. He craves order;

that's what he looks for in the universe, when he hunts out formal gardens. He will have made floors and walls, doors and rooms. He will have found a place to put everything.

Room:

place space area capacity territory expanse area length width breadth building site spot dwelling den

Rooms, yes: there have been so many rooms. Walking through them and sitting in them. In my basement I worked amongst the flowers that had been pressed into discs and filed on the oak racks that lined the walls. The room where my father died was in a hospice, a building coated in magnolia paint, the only other colour provided by a silk spray of pink carnations in a tall vase by his bedside. Bottles of pills clustered around it. The Royal Albert Hall was a grand room; Beethoven's ninth symphony was up to the task of filling it. Graham and I were sitting far to the left, in cheap seats, peripheral to the sound and yet included, incorporated, alive within it.

There are far too many connections to hold, but I swell with them until I feel my seams straining.

Then I reach out, and pull at the room until it shifts, and becomes a new box, a fresh page, the next panel in this comic strip.

EGGS

It's warm and dark, a relief to my eyes after so much brightness. At first I'm only aware of the soft, ruddy light seeping through the porous, curved walls that have closed around me.

An egg. Am I in an egg? Or maybe a womb. Everything is cushioned and contained, and I feel very far from the outside, whatever that is. There's a low sound, a murmur: rhythmic, soporific.

My eyes adjust. It's small. There's barely room to move. But when I extend an arm to touch the wall – which pulses, and looks spongy, wet – it is not within my reach. I lean forward, then take a step. Another. I start walking, and the wall ahead of me grows a dark central line, and then parts to form a corridor that moves with me. So I carry on walking and it carries on growing. I feel safe. I feel very little.

It would be so easy to let everything leave me. I could walk forever and get nowhere. I stop, suddenly uneasy, and sit on the floor, which gives a little under my weight. It is bouncy and stretched, like a trampoline.

In the stillness, in the *shush-shush* sounds, I realise I'm not alone.

Their presence is not frightening. They are in the darkness, collected, floating. They move towards me, and they are very small; they have to draw close before I can make out that they are almost human in their appearance, little bodies curled up tight, bald heads bent to flexed knees, spines curled. Their skin has a delicate, transparent quality that I have seen on the very young and the very old. I am so homesick. But the human part of me is so much smaller than it was.

These little creatures are not human. Their vertebrae give them away. Each one pokes out from their rice paper skin to reveal not bone, but wood. Their spines are branches. Some even grow buds, tiny red leaves. They are trees, in some way. They are as sweet and strong and wise and old and young as trees.

They are close enough to touch me, but I can't feel it as they jostle against my skin. All their eyes are closed and their mouths open. They smell clean and green, like dew. I think they're asleep, aware of me only in their dreams.

They must be the Cynarans.

Sealed up in this warm, safe space, they are dormant. They don't have real bodies, but to me they are visible as possibilities of life. Both foetal and decrepit, both plant and animal. They hover, they cuddle up, they are attracted to me, and I, in turn, feel protective of them.

They remind me of the time I carried Lily, and often imagined her wrapped up tight this way, inside me. It's hard to connect these beings to Hort at all, even though I know he is one of them. Hort makes me feel very different things, now.

It's easy to put those feelings aside once more and enjoy the explorations of the Cynarans against my skin. They keep jostling and bouncing off. There are hundreds of them, at least thirty in my lap alone, between my crossed legs. But although they cannot sink into me they can penetrate each other, their skins sliding so they overlap and lock, then pull apart those fine membranous layers. I wonder what they're sharing when that happens.

How different my life would have been – the path of humanity might have been – if we'd perfected that trick. To not be so unrelentingly separate.

If I could wake the Cynarans up, what would they do?

Would they communicate with me? Want to know about Hort and his travels? Would they condemn him?

The truth is that this is yet another life form that I have no hope of understanding. But I like them. And I get the wild and unsubstantiated feeling that they like me.

I'm definitely not brave enough to put that to the test, and wake them up.

I stand up and they scatter, are gone in a heartbeat.

I pull myself to the next room.

MAPS

From a snug sanctuary to the chilly night sky – is this Earth? Of course not; it couldn't be. Earth is lost to green sludge and this place has plants everywhere I look: beautiful oaks in the distance, and a row of poplars behind which stands an old farmhouse, the windows lit and welcoming. All around me wheat is springing from the soil. I'm standing in it. It's nearly up to my hands in height, and it is having a good year. it looks strong, green-gold and nearly ready for harvest.

I feel more like myself again.

Wheat – Triticum aestivum – is such a complex combination of natural bounty and human interference. It has been bred and modified since we first became farmers to yield more, to be bigger, to be faster, and for that reason I've long admired it, much as I admired dogs and horses for their ability to adapt to suit us, thereby ensuring their own survival. I stroke the ears and a breeze picks up and sways the stalks against me. This is a huge field; it could feed thousands.

Bread. I miss bread. A stabbing sensation in my stomach informs me that I should eat, but it's much like breathing, like living. It's not really me any more.

And, with that thought, the wheat explodes.

The ears fire straight up, each one accompanied by a soft popping sound, and the grains spread across the night. They hang there. They do not fall. They create a pattern, glowing, visible, like dots from a silver pen on black paper.

I begin to discern familiar shapes, as is human nature. We search for a face in everything, I read that once. Faces in toast, in toilets, in clouds, in cornflakes. I see a face that I love: Lily, eyes bright, mouth turned up a little, nose very straight in seven adjacent stars. The star at the tip of her nose is bigger than the rest. I stare at it, wondering what it really is outside of my imagination, and I hear in my head, in my own voice, very calm and composed, the word:

Cynara

I look at the mark above, and the voice says:

Onopordum

Planets. I'm looking at a map of the universe. I turn to my attention to each one that makes up Lily's nose:

Carduus

Sonchus

Cicerbita

Cnicus

Echinops

All thistles. A family of planets, of plants, mingled together by my attempt to understand something that is utterly beyond me.

There are so many stars, far too many to collect all their names.

I return my attention to Cynara. Where all the other dots are white, it has started to glow green.

Senescence. The virus at its origin point. This is not just a map, it is a record of an event, and the beginning of a story.

I watch the planet become a vivid green, and then turn black. It is no longer visible in the night sky.

But the virus has moved. What did Hort say in the last scrolling saga he put in my head? The Cynarans moved to a nearby planet, and now I can see it attacking Onopordum. The green is upon it. I'm watching the death of that planet, too. The life forms get swamped by the disease and Onopordum goes dark.

Hort said that at this point the Cynarans put themselves to sleep. But he did not: where next? To what star did he journey? I scan the map and see it. Another dot is turning green. Then another. Another, all happening too fast for me to focus upon them and learn their names. Onwards, and onwards. Here, and here, and here, and gone. Gone. How could Hort have been so cruel? He knew what he was doing.

I can't bear to watch any more.

I turn away, and pull at the seam of the room until the page is turned.

BOXES (GREENBEARD)

A plain room, as tall as it is wide, without doors or windows, the walls off-white. In the far corner there's a stack of those cardboard boxes Hort makes, forming a pyramid. I walk to them, hearing my footsteps echo on the tiled floor. Everything here is a square or a cube. The walls bear barely visible grey lines, running horizontally and vertically. It's disorientating.

At first I think, *another storage area, a literal box room*. But Hort already has one of those, and I've seen it – shelves stacked high with trinkets he has taken from the places he has visited and massacred.

Cardboard boxes are so very reminiscent of home.

Good things come in them. It's a prejudice of mine that's hard to overcome. My seeds would often arrive sealed in plastic, wrapped in cotton wool, closed up in a very small cardboard box to protect them on their journey to reach me. It seemed to me, once upon a time, that those seeds were making an incredibly long and arduous trip. Now I know that seeds can cross a universe. My own Collection is in a cardboard box again, close by.

Christmas presents, too, and books, clothes, things ordered off the internet: they all came in cardboard boxes. This could be a room of pleasant surprises. Perhaps that's what my mind is trying to tell me by presenting the information in this form.

I'm trying to justify the act of opening one, I know it.

I'm building myself up to it.

To be fair, bad things also come in boxes. I saw a film – I can't remember the name – where a madman cut off the head of a police detective's wife and mailed it to him, in a box. I remember thinking it was unrealistic – the box would have leaked, surely? What on earth was it lined with? I said as much to Graham after we left the cinema; it was a comment designed to annoy him. It had been his choice of film, and I rather resented the darkness of it. I would have preferred a comedy, but instead he had reached out to this violent fantasy, had responded to it, and I could see he had lost himself within it, thinking it represented some sort of truth about the world that I didn't choose to share.

None of these boxes are dripping, thank goodness.

I don't pick up the one that sits right at the top – the apex box. For a start, I'd need a stepladder to reach it. The pyramid is at least a couple of feet taller than I am, and I'd estimate there are over two hundred boxes. So I pick one at random, level with my waist, and slide it free. Nothing tumbles down; this is a solid construction. Behind the box I've removed sit more boxes. Hort must have built this with care.

So he doesn't always destroy everything. That's good to know.

Straight away I can tell that the box I'm holding is not empty. It contains something small and light, but there's a definite weight to it. I shake it, just a little, and it shifts from side to side. The memory of Christmases past is too strong to overcome.

The lid is made of four leaves of cardboard folded over each other. I prise them apart, and look inside.

It's a plant.

An aloe vera.

I lift it free of the box. It's not in the best condition, although I should simply be surprised that it's alive at all, considering it gets no sun and no water, and who knows how long its been here, packed away in the pyramid? It's been potted in a small ceramic holder, one of those generic ones garden centres use en masse. A quick glance at the bottom of the pot confirms my suspicions: the aloe vera is rootbound. Faint, spidery protusions of the plant have squeezed their way out through the four small holes drilled there. It urgently needs repotting; my fingers itch to find a bigger home for it. I need a trowel, water, some good earth.

Poor little plant.

I've always loved the leaves of the aloe vera, with the sharp blade giving way to a fleshy base and thick petiole. I stroke a finger along one, and the plant whispers in response. It has a voice that is soft and high and secretive, and it says:

I should never have gone, I should have known better but there were promises, and the things! The things I've seen! There was a hard land of diamond and beings of gas, and somehow it all made sense to me, for a little while, until I couldn't hold it all within me and it changed to a roaring, endless darkness, and I can't remember why, I can't remember why. But I have to save them, that's the idea, there are so many to be saved, including— I can't— I can't recall—

I take my hand from the leaf and the whispering stops.

Good and bad things come in boxes.

I can't bring myself to return the aloe vera to that small, dark space, to be sealed and stacked. I put it down, by my feet, and reach for another box. To check. To be certain.

This time there's a calathea inside. It's known colloquially as the peacock plant, and the name suits it; it has round, elegant markings on its feathery leaves, shades of light and dark green with a blush of pink on the undersides. It's in another one of those little pots. I never liked those little pots.

I put a trembling finger on one of the leaves. The voice is loud, confident, filling the room:

Back home there were stories of a plague that travelled through the stars looking for the keepers of the secrets of the growing worlds, and I thought it was a myth meant to focus us on our tasks, to help us recognise the importance of what we did and why we should protect the trees that we trimmed and shaped to house and nourish our young. Symbiosis, of course, although I didn't recognise it in those terms until I was much older, which is ironic for time has not actually passed and yet I'm ancient and will never give up a child to a tree, now. What a waste. What a waste of me, but when the plague came to my town and charmed me, made a course straight for me, I thought it was going to be the making of me. I taught her my songs, and she said, Greetings! There may be answers here, answers to terrible puzzles, let me show you, and I went. I cannot remember my songs now. I said to her, my songs are gone, teach them back to me, and she said, there is no point, you won't retain it now, you are broken, you are no good to me in pieces. I want to relearn my songs. Teach me my songs.

I put the calathea down, next to the aloe vera.

Should I nudge them closer to each other, so they are touching? Or would that be cruel? I don't think they can listen. I suspect it would be a meaningless act. This is not communication, but a fragment of a part of what was a soul. A personality. The few pieces that remain, gathered up, and placed in a handy container.

I pick up another box.

It's a fern, which is a grand old plant, in evolutionary terms. A Japanese tassel. Polystichum polyblepharum. The voice sounds older too, with a rich, sedate tone, the words slower, placed carefully in order:

It was the festival of Thanks for the Breeze when the Gardener arrived, and asked me to come with it on a journey through the stars. It was very beautiful, and I was in love. We entwined antennae and I gave it my vestigial limbs to eat, as is our custom; these thoughts and feelings are as clear to me now as then and I have not lost them, for which I am grateful. I have agreed to be stored and contained, as I am beyond help, beyond finding myself, and I do not wish to lose any more of what have been magnificent times together, for so long, to countless worlds that burned green for us, because of us, and died when we left them. Every one of them was a monument to our... companionship and we danced in that knowledge. Let this be the last thought I hold as I am stacked away with the others who came before – and there will be more, there will be more – I have loved without fear, without restraint, without... morality or judgement. That is who I will remain. I have no need of a name.

I put the fern with the other plant, and start to open more boxes, touch more pot plants, hear more stories. I can't stop.

Hort is described in many ways by these voices, but I can always tell that they are talking about him. Him to me, she or it or they to others, and sometimes there are long pauses as the limitations of language are reached. Hort has been a lover, a murderer, an adventurer, a cataclysm, a god. But to him we have all been the trusty companion.

And we end up here, packed away when we are too fragmented to be of any use. He pops us in little boxes and seals each one shut, and goes out to find another companion to traipse across the universe with him. We have all given him something unique, I suspect. Not one pot plant is repeated.

But in the end we are all still just pot plants.

I wonder, if I make a real effort, if I could see these pot plants for the beings they really are. Or, at least, what's left of them.

I find I don't want to do that.

I survey the many pot plants on the floor, knowing I will not be able to stack them away, and add my voices to theirs:

"I will not end up this way," I tell them.

I don't know if I will have any choice in the matter, but I say it anyway.

Then I find the edges of the room, and pull.

ARCHIVES

It's a terrible thing, to find out how unimportant you really are.

The universe is vast, yes, and there are billions of beings, of meanings, of stories out there. I must admit that my head was turned by the idea of being important on that grand scale, when Hort first came along. It's not the loss of that notion that hurts.

It's the fact that I'm not even important in my own story. I am the one wearing a red shirt. I am expendable.

I truly am a pot plant.

But I'm also still human, at least in thoughts, to some extent, and it's impossible not to feel things in response to this place, which is not new to me, not by any means.

I'm in a museum that I've visited before, in one of my favourite cities in the world.

I'm in Turin.

Turin is wonderful. I visited it soon after the divorce. Graham took care of Lily for the first time on his own. She was twelve, and I remember feeling such guilt and terror at the thought of leaving her. But once I had arrived, and checked in at the small hotel not far from the Piazza Statuto, I sat in a cafe, ordered espresso, and felt such concepts drain from me utterly. Instead there was only relief that I could not have suppressed. It demanded to be identified as *freedom*, although I hated that word. I didn't crave liberation, at least, not from Lily, and Graham had let me go with a disturbing ease, having been aware far earlier than me that my heart really wasn't in it.

What I craved, and what I was in Turin for, was one and the same thing: the viola cryana.

A small wild pansy of France with thick, dark green leaves in which light mauve flowers hid, the viola cryana had been thought extinct since the 1920s, although many botanists had tried to locate it since, searching around limestone hills throughout Europe. It was not being hunted for any reason in particular. Sometimes it's simply the act of being gone that makes something seem special.

Certainly that was what made it worth pursuing for me, when I first read in a gardening magazine about a secretive Italian nursery just outside Turin that claimed to have found and successfully bred viola cryanas.

They did not have a telephone number that I could find. I wrote to them, in longhand, and received no reply. It seemed a perfectly reasonable request to me. I wanted to preserve the flower, if they truly had it, which I couldn't quite believe. The viola cryana: it was not particularly beautiful or blessed with a magnificent scent, but it had been gone for good. Could it really have simply been hiding, all this time? It represented hope, perhaps. I wanted it to keep on representing that, even if only within my Collection.

I hired a car and drove to the nursery, and they were perfectly pleasant when showing me around their rows of alpines and succulents, but as soon as I mentioned the viola

I was shown the door. They weren't interested in reason, or in money, which I offered in desperation.

That was what persuaded me that they really did have it.

So I drove back in the dead of night, broke into that aging, unguarded greenhouse, and took one. It was small, lopsided, a bright purple petal that faded where it tenuously attached to the pistil.

I should be ashamed of that crime. Am I, though? Am I ashamed?

I look back at it now and it seems so clear to me that I relished being placed in the situation where I could justify such behaviour: the bank would not be complete without it; I had to commit the crime for the sake of the whole planet; I was the only one who could possibly safeguard a diverse and healthy plant-filled future.

How much fun it is, to be on moral high ground. How easily it makes bad behaviour good.

I felt no such introspection on the afternoon before my heist. There was only excitement and inevitability. I visited the museum I'm now standing in (not the real one, I know I'm not standing in the *real* one) and strolled around the exhibits, thinking it might distract me. It was a good choice, being a magnificent building with a spiritual central space, well-proportioned, in semi-darkness. A bell tower high above could be reached – appropriately enough for a space dedicated to flights of filmic fancy – by a ride in a glass elevator.

The Museo Nazionale del Cinema.

Screens have been set up, each one showing a clip of a film, some in vivid rolling Technicolor and some in jerky, crackling black and white. There are no signs to explain what they mean, although that fact is obvious to me: they are moments from Hort's life.

In the real museum long explanations of why each clip had been chosen as an important cinematic event had been posted to the wall beside each screen. But they were in Italian, without translation, and so I had watched each clip on its own terms, feeling my own emotions about each face, every action and reaction shot, cut and close-up, track and pan. Film is its own language, too, and the same is true of the scenes I'm watching now. I can translate them as telling me one major thing:

Hort is his own hero.

I walk around the museum and watch him, always in the centre of the screen looking handsome and looking brave, looking athletic, manly, and yet sensitive, intelligent, even a little kooky with his bright green shoes and quirky eyebrows.

The assistants are always in shot too, behind him or next to him, not quite in focus. They stay close, listen when he talks, run when he runs. They come in all shapes and sizes, have varying amounts of eyes, arms, beaks, humps, feelers, protrusions, carapaces, wings. Even so, they are all easily identifiable to me as the assistants. It's to do with their position on the screen.

Moving from clip to clip, pausing in front of each one, I observe Hort's daring deeds. He leaps, he sprints, he charms, he saves. Eventually I reach a clip in which I recognise myself in the background. It's Tearthumb, the colours looking brighter, the limbtrees weirder. Hort is talking to Fluffy the flamingo. They are discussing their plan to overthrow the Tyrants.

It'll never work, says Fluffy.

Trust me, says Hort. *I know what I'm doing. This is going to work out swimmingly.*

I watch the clip over and over. Would he really have used the word 'swimmingly'? Or is that only my interpretation of what happened? I don't know. This moment, captured, is not truthful. It is a representation, a slick shiny spin. But then, how is that different from what I told myself at the time? We were on a planet helping flamingos fight lizards. We were adventurers, we were partners, there was a hint of romance between us. It was all as ridiculous as only a human imagination can be.

That's what it boils down to, isn't it? I'm so human.

I'm still human, even with the bits that are lost, with the holes I can't fill. Even without a working body and chestnut growing inside the bits that are left, I'm human. Even blown apart into a million pieces of information rather than being a biological organism, even outside of time itself; I see it all a certain way.

Just as Hort sees his life as a film, and his role as a star.

There are far too many clips to watch them all, so I only stop in front of the ones that catch my attention. Even though I'm walking in circles, the clips never repeat. I'm on a loop in this darkness, listening to Hort's voice as he reassures and persuades and cajoles on a thousand planets. If they came with a title, they would read:

Hort defeats the monster!
Hort escapes death!
Hort narrowly avoids disaster!
Hort charms the locals!
A Victory Parade for Hort!

And so on.

If the credits ever rolled, I would see, in very small letters:

Featuring a cast of indigenous beings and a trained pot plant.

The bit that reads:

No animals were harmed during the making of this motion picture.

Well. That wouldn't be there.

Eventually, just like with the other rooms, I tire of being here. I don't want to see his exploits any more. I want to have ones of my own.

I signed up to save the world, didn't I?

CLOCKED

Back in the glass room, with the steeple high above and the uniform grey of nothingness pretending to be clouds outside, I lie on the floor because I don't know how to make a single bed appear.

Maybe I should sleep. Sleep for as long as it takes until he returns.

But my thoughts won't switch off. One thought in particular, in fact, and it's not a helpful one:

The peri-menopause was a horrible business.

It's not relevant to anything.

Wait. Yes it is. Insomnia. The inability to sleep. There are many other symptoms when it comes to the peri-menopause, of course, and I had a lot of them, such as the mood swings, the joint pains, the hot flushes, the thinning of the hair on my head and the thickening of the hair on my top lip and chin. A cluster of discomforts. Is that the collective noun for discomfort? An irritability. A nuisance. None of these words come close to describing what it's like to live every moment of every day with small ailments that soon add up to a much large issue. I used to wake up at three o'clock in the morning and could never get back to sleep until five o'clock at the earliest. I would spend those two hours in front of the open fridge door, or standing in the garden, knowing it was cold and not feeling it. I should have felt it. My skin was icy to touch, but inside I burned with the awareness of my time as a fertile woman running out.

Then it switched off. I was cool and unbothered again. There was no more blood and heat. The sheets did not form a sticky tangle around my thickening waist and legs in the witching hours.

Lily was at university, then, studying mathematics.

I just want to understand.

She burned, too, in a different way, I could see the flame in her whenever she came home from the holidays. I wonder if I was the same, at that age.

I look down at my body. The years have accumulated upon it as inches, as folds, as a change in contours, in texture, in trajectory.

Youth:

juvenescence immaturity freshness springtime nonage infancy babyhood growth beginning eruption commencement innocence smoothness possibility

Putting my hands to my brittle hair, my face, my sagging neck, the soft comforting weight of my breasts, the three rolls of my stomach leading to the finer ripples of my thighs. My hefty, cylindrical knees.

Power is growing in me.

I know how to do this. It's in the words. I can make the words work. I take off all that is old, and used, and accumulated. I strip back to the age of first burning, and I can feel the change. I don't need a mirror to know that it's worked.

It makes me feel closer to Lily than I have done in a long time. It's almost as good as being with her for a while. It's almost like being her.

I walk around, enjoying the difference in my hips, the muscles of my arms and legs. How firm I am at this age. Nothing rubs together. I'm strong and tall, like a tree.

Except that my feet still hurt.

I slip off my trusty court shoes. A pair of feet that still belong to a fifty-three-year-old woman confront me, with yellowing toenails and curved big toes, and shooting pains down both tired arches when I plant them flat on the floor.

Actually, I like it. I feel comfortable in my old feet. I'll leave them as they are. I wouldn't want to be completely young again. This way, the part of me that is grounded will stay wise and weighty.

Now I have the trick of it, I go further and summon some grasses, bentgrass and slender creeping red fescue, to produce a soft, fine-leaved lawn underfoot into which I can wiggle my toes. Being old and young at the same time is a delight. I am a little bit of my father, and a little bit of my daughter. I'm so much more human this way; I encompass both ends of the experience. A perfect lawn is never quite right to me, so I summon some daisies. That's better. Then some trefoil, which loves to creep into the great British lawn and weave its way through the blades. Then digitaria – crabgrass. A real pest if you want only beautiful leaves on your lawn, but I like the texture this time. These are some of the first plants my father collected with the Vice; I suppose they were a trial run, just to see if it worked. He picked whatever was close to hand. Clover and chickweed too, and then the dandelion.

Dandelion: that rings a bell. One of the Rampion's memories surfaces, demands attention. Dandelion was the name of the body-hopping creature he sent to Earth to deliver the Vice.

Dandelions are such interesting flowers, often called a weed, and yet it can be cultivated for eating and its bright yellow head has often been a welcome sight to me in the morning. An asexual plant, it does not pollinate. Each flower is genetically identical to the parent plant. They are often overlooked as unimportant.

Hort thought the Rampion's employee was unimportant too, compared to his mission to save the universe from himself.

I think about the humble dandelion, all the words that can be weaved around it, and I grow one.

It's not a plant that springs from the floor. It's a boy. His body erupts, feet and head together, bent over double, and then he uncurls from the waist and his arms spread from two nubs, stretching out, reaching up. His face is a round disc, alight with a smile, eyes screwed tight shut, turned up to the steeple. His hair is a sunny gold, standing out in fine spikes from the crown of his head. Naked, he is beautiful and fresh and everything of youth that I had imagined for myself. He puts me to shame. He is vivacity personified.

His legs remain rooted to the floor but, apart from that, he seems very human to me. He's a boy. Just like any boy. His eyes open. They are light grey, and somehow empty of thought – it's in the way he does not look around him, or see me at all. He's not really here in the room with me. I open my mouth to speak, but he beats me to it, and once he starts he does not stop:

I made the decision in a moment between others, with nothing to delineate it as noteworthy; we were having a discussion about a Mr Darwin, and how a voyage can be the making of both a man and a methodology. I told you, Francis, of my own voyages and how I still sail them, in different vessels, where time is not the master of me as it is of you and your kind, and your mouth opened wide at such an idea.

I cannot bear to leave you. See, I make the decision again, just the same. I have stayed, and been shrunken to a disc, for you.

I have enjoyed speaking about your scientists, and all our other truly irrelevant conversations. The ones I like best are when you describe the unfolding of personal motivation as if it is the solving of a mystery. The way you live with so little knowledge is what makes me happiest.

Staying here, with you, is a surprise to me. The only surprise of my life, in fact, yet all future and past aligned anew with it as the horizon on my travels as soon as it was made, and the way it was meant to be before that moment was lost to me.

It's the closest I will ever get to being human.

I hope you are proud of me.

Dear Francis,

Here is the beginning of what I wanted to say to you. I knew it was in here somewhere. I must sort through what is left after the compression to find myself. I hope I'm doing a reasonable job of that.

Do I seem familiar to you?

I have taught you all you need to know to use the Vice, and I have explained to you why it is important. I would say to you simply – *capture the flowers!* – if I was the order-giving type but I know how often an order ignites only rebellion, not compliance. Besides, I have never wanted to be the commander of you, but please allow me, Francis, to respectfully suggest… well, you have heard this before and I have said it before.

Goodbye, then. I am bound to you and now and still and anew. I feel certain of it. Goodbye, from your little lion.

The ending came upon me suddenly, there, rather more quickly than I was expecting, and I still have things to say. The confusions of living the linear life!

What next?

What next?

You said, *I'm sorry, are you talking to me?*

I said, *Stop acting the fool, we have work to do, what kind of flower is this?*

You said, *I'm afraid I don't know.*

And I realised: this is our first meeting, before you knew a thing about why we were, would be, together. I have never stood in your presence before but I know that mouth so well. Your talking mouth and the words you say are stamped all over me and my journeys. *I see the future*, I said to you, once, twice, more, because that is the easiest way to explain it. *My present actions are not in thrall to the past.*

Waterbeach is a pleasant village, but you tell me you have plans to relocate. *Why?* I ask, and you laugh as if I couldn't possibly understand. To you I am a small boy whom you found standing next to you in a field of wild flowers not far from a runway, and you assumed I was like you. That I had come to see planes take off and land.

I'm still not sure what a plane is.

You said, in the act of attempting to explain it, you said:

RAF Waterbeach is an Air Force Station located about, oh, I'd say five miles north of Cambridge? Lancasters flew from here during the war, and my father was a navigator back then, sitting behind the pilot, separated off by a small curtain so he could concentrate on his charts. He said he never once looked out over the view from up in the sky. Always with his nose down in the charts.

How does this explain planes to me? Even so, I like the way your mouth moves with animation when you speak of them. I also see pain in your words, folded up carefully within each one, but you never unpack them to reveal their contents and so, to you, this suitcase is not heavy. Such joy in things that fly, are light, but now I've laden you with the Vice and the task. I even suggest that it will not be a task you finish in your lifetime, and you can pass it on to the next. The child. The one who comes after me, and is visible in your future.

The year is 1956, you tell me.

I don't know what that means.

When do I have a child? What year? Will he be like you?

I laugh as if you couldn't possibly understand.

I know it has hurt you deeply to reduce me to a disc, but it is the only way I could stay, and you could keep your Collection.

I'm filled with the way you said, *Where are your parents?*

I'm alone, I said. I'm saying. I continue to say.

You keep notes in a small book, like Darwin did. You call it a diary.

For that first day you described me as *a lost child.* You thought I was innocence, interrupted. But then you, now you, know me better.

It's better not to tell the child everything, I said. *No good comes of telling everyone everything.*

Don't tell me how to raise my own child. Particularly one that hasn't even been born yet. Which is a good point, isn't it? Yes. A good point. *Who is the mother, anyway? How will I know her when I see her?*

She's not important, I said. *She doesn't stay.*

I regret those words.

For the look on your face, the shape your mouth made as you shouted in your brute language, blunt words. At me?

Near me.

At the things I knew and you didn't. Don't want to. Know.

Hello, Francis. It's me.

We are back to the start.

My way of commencing conversations in the middle and departing before the end never stops taking you by surprise, does it? Here is the moment where I explain that I am from a different planet. It's a wonderful moment, because you were eating soup and I made you slurp.

What planet? you ask me.

What difference does it make? But I take you outside, leading you by the hand, and point out a star in the sky.

A random one, but you enjoy the experience. You imbue it with meaning it does not have.

You love to look up.

But at our first meeting I said, *What kind of flower is this?*

And you looked down at the ground for me.

You took me home and heated soup.

I suppose you can stay here tonight, you said. *I'll contact the authorities and they can try to find your family.*

But I'm alone.

I keep saying it.

Before you put me through the Vice, after our longest argument, you said, *You have given me a taste for fatherhood, my Leo. You have been a wonderful son.*

I was annoyed by your need to slap your light, trite words on my emotions, but I know you have no other tools at your disposal.

Actions speak louder than words, said the voice from the radio, and you wondered why I laughed so much.

It's meant to be a drama, Leo, you said.

Dear Francis,

I am not Leo any more. I am a compression of the information that comprised Leo, which was in itself a creation of your imagination to make sense of what I am. There are benefits and drawbacks to my new disc life.

I will leave you to decide which is which.

- I feel nothing.
- I create nothing.
- I cannot seed, nor fly free.
- I cannot take root.
- I cannot *see the future* any more. Such a quaint phrase that completely fails to grasp the situation; you took to it immediately, though, and asked me often, *Did you see that? In the future?*
  Like son, like father.
- I am not alive.
- I cannot die.
- I am of and in this moment.
- I belong to you.

I sit on your shelves as part of your collection, and I already know you will not find me. There is, from now on, a long silence.

Anyway, I have muddled up this conversation. I'm sorry, Francis.

I know it makes things difficult to follow.

To continue:

You're a plant?

A photosynthentic being.

Planes, plants, planets. So much in common.

You swapped your planes for two new obsessions: the night sky above, and the ground below.

Stars and flowers.

Thank you very much for letting me stay, I said.

You said, *Yes, well, your case looks very heavy. Do you want me to take it upstairs for you? I have a box room in the attic you can use, for now.*

Waterbeach is a village close to an RAF base where bombers flew from in the war. It is roughly five miles north of Cambridge. I fell there by chance, and took a body that was a shape you would love.

You call this shape a boy.

This is all entirely random and I have always known you.

I opened the suitcase and showed you the Vice.

I told you it was wrapped in invisible space-transporting string.

Goodness, you said. *I don't understand what that is.*

And so, dear Francis, I reach the end of this recording and recollection, sorting and rewinding.

To remember:

You believed me, although I could tell you very little and you could grasp even less. I asked you to collect flowers, and you said, *yes.*

You offered to adopt me, and I said, *I am already your child.*

And you said, *yes.*

Your mouth moves in a certain way for that word. I have practised it, in boy form, in front of a mirror. I want to look like you.

How will collecting the flowers help? you said, after I showed you how to use the Vice for the first time.

There comes a time when the Collection saves you.

This is another horrible simplification, forgive me, forgive me. I must use words within our limitations.

He falls silent. His eyes close.

He shrivels, his head tucking into his body, his spine drooping, his arms falling from his body to float to the floor. He dies like a dandelion starved of sunshine, turning black and brittle and then withering away, leaving only a stain on the floor, which then returns to white.

I must get back to Earth.

That's the thought in my head, the shout that is drowning everything else out.

I miss my father so very much. I know him better now. He was a distant man, yes. His head was in the stars, his eyes were on the ground, and his heart was in his Collection.

Everything else is still inexplicable, but that matters less. What does it affect, how I choose to see everything? How much of it I can follow? The Collection will save him. It can't possibly save him, since he's already dead, but it saves someone. Why not Lily? Why not the seed of his seed? Wouldn't that make sense to a creature who saw the future? It's far from the most ridiculous thing I've chosen to believe.

I don't just miss my father.

I miss Earth, like never before. I belong to Earth. I belong on it. And so do my flowers.

LILY, WITHERING

Lily: It's an important day. We didn't want it to pass without saying something. Something that feels permanent. Dad, do you want to go first?

Graham: Yes, okay.

[Pause.]

Graham: I don't really know how to start.

Lily: We dug out the basement.

Graham: Yes. We dug out the basement. It got easier as time went on because the swamp continued to dry, and by the time we finished it was turning to a chalky substance, black and brittle, flakey. We scraped the last of it up with our hands. There was no sign of the Collection, but on the floor, on the floor there was a body.

Lily: The body of Penelope
Greensmith.

Graham: Yes, her body. The, um, the
swamp had kept her, um, intact.
I mean, it was definitely her,
there's no doubt in my mind.

Lily: She was wearing her usual
cardigan.

Graham: The swamp preserved her. Is
that the right word? There's no
sign of what— what caused her
death.

Lily: But with Grandad's Collection
and the Vice gone, we have to
assume it was a— an attack—

Graham: A criminal. She would have
fought for that Collection.
Particularly with what's been
happening now. She would have
fought hard.

Lily: It doesn't make any sense.

[Pause.]

Graham: No, but nothing does any more,
does it? Except this. Except me
and you. And your Mum, she's
been here all along, with us,
hasn't she? She didn't leave you
behind.

Lily: She was in the basement the
         whole time. That's where she
         liked to be.

Graham: Sleep well, Pen. It might not be
         too long before we see you
         again.

Lily: You want me to turn it off?

Graham: Yes, I'm done.

[Pause.]

Lily: Well, I'm not.

[Pause.]

Lily: I don't want to say sweet words
         about this, and pretend that I'm
         not angry. I'm incredibly
         angry. I just want to
         understand. How can she have
         been in the basement the
         entire time? I thought I could
         feel a connection. That she
         was out there, somewhere. We
         weren't very close, but surely
         the fact that she was my mother
         meant that I would know when
         she was dead? When she was
         under a swamp? I don't think I
         knew her at all.

Graham: Sweetie, it's not—

Lily: No. No. I didn't know her at all. And she didn't know me. She had some memories in her head, at least, of when I was little and cute and easy to hug, and when she thought of me, she probably thought of that because that's easier than thinking about the adult version, and the fact that we barely saw each other because we didn't really like each other. But I don't have a memory of those days, so I can't choose to prioritise those memories over reality. I'll end up remembering digging out her body with my bare hands. Lovely. That's my abiding memory.

Graham: That will fade. I promise you.

Lily: That will fade in time before we both die too?

[Pause.]

Graham: Possibly not.

Lily: No. Possibly not. I'm tired. I think I'll turn in.

THE RETURN OF...

He's a mass murderer, a virus, a liar, a narcissist and the man who has condemned my daughter and my planet to death, unless I think up a solution. Which I haven't been able to do so far. But when a doorway appears in the Storage Room, interrupting my cataloguing, and Hort tumbles through it, I go to him. I hold him. He feels alive. He is flesh to me.

His lungs expand and contract within the circle of my arms as he hugs me back. I know that's not true. He doesn't have lungs. Right now, he's a person to me. He's as close as I can get to a person. It's been so long. An unbearable amount of long.

I'm crying.

"Pea," he breathes, and I melt into him, his smell, the way he makes me the centre of his universe.

I can't break the hug. I can't be that cruel to myself.

He's breathing hard when we break apart – I know, I know, not true – and whispers, "I missed you." So close I can see his skin is not perfect. He looks tired; his eyes are drawn and his cheeks are dry, reddened. A small frown forms, just a crease between his eyebrows. "Something's different. Don't tell me."

He honestly can't place it.

"I'm young."

"You're young," he repeats. "Look at that. And you've managed to negotiate the rooms, by the look of you."

"I have."

"Well," he says. "Then you know all my secrets."

"I don't think anyone knows all your secrets."

"But you understand me a little better, don't you? Please say you do, Pea. That's what I want. That's what I've always wanted."

Loneliness. Time that does not pass. The choice of sleep or isolation is so very difficult to make, particularly when there is much to see, many lives to touch.

Except touching them means killing them.

"I don't think I'll ever understand you," I tell him.

He flinches, then finds a smile. "Well," he says. "No. There's probably not enough time for that." He deepens his inflexion on the word *time*, and shakes his head. The connections float forth: I see them, I actually see them as objects. They are the achenes of a dandelion clock, blown free by a child. How appropriate.

Time:

point past second instance juncture moment present age date day season lifetime shift span tempo term turning week while year hour life era age extent continuance duration epoch eternity

I gather them all up in my hands and sort them into an order that makes sense to me, in terms of the time Hort and I have spent together. I put *present* on the top of the pile, then give it to him. He takes it and squashes it between his palms, then pulls me back into his arms and hugs me again.

I love it. I love his enjoyment in holding me. I mirror it. I want only to feel it, to be part of it. I will be his mirror.

"Incredible," he says, "that there's any of you left. I thought you'd all be gone by now. Moving around in here, learning to manipulate things, has a high cost. Have you noticed you're forgetting things?" Then he steps back and looks around the storage room. "You've done it through cataloguing, haven't you? My clever Pea. You're sorting everything. Including yourself. That should help you to hold it together for a little longer."

It's true. I've learned how to use the storage room, and its strange ability to bring the objects Hort has collected on his travels, by ordering my thoughts and placing associations in my mind. I have looked through countless items, most of which make no sense to me, and have treated them like my flowers, finding ways to describe each one in terms of their possible usefulness for saving the universe. Now, when I think of certain things, a corresponding object appears. Does it matter if I'm making up my own definitions? Not any longer. Not to me.

But perhaps it's all been pointless. By the sound of it, I won't be around for much longer anyway.

"Did it give you a cure?"

"The Armillaria? It's an interesting being. It offered me a trade."

"What kind of trade?" I ask him. I don't like the way he's talking about this, making light of it. It's easier when we're talking and not touching to remember that I don't trust him. Not any more.

"It's a gatekeeper, of a sort. There are a few of them left. They hold up boundaries, to stop it all bleeding together through a process they call 'universalisation'. By keeping us all separate, diversification can be safeguarded. We don't all want to end up as the same being, after all! Think of it as protection of the weak. But, yes, this one understood my problem and offered me a one-time offer of passage to a different universe. One that has already fully senesced, so there would be nothing for me to affect. But, you know, Pea – look at you! You're holding yourself together beautifully! I never thought I'd be able to say this to a companion, but... We can go together, my darling. Imagine, a whole new universe to play in. One without hunger, or fear, or pain. You might even call it..." His mouth moves without producing a sound, and then I hear the word: *Heaven.*

"Heaven?" I repeat. Heaven.

Hort touches my forehead with the back of his hand. "Are you okay? Don't get stressed out. You're losing it."

"Losing it?"

"Your control. I'm making you angry, somehow, aren't I? I'm sorry. But we should find a way to work through it. I can't help but make you angry sometimes, right? You need to hold yourself – what's left of you – together."

"Is that what went wrong with your other pot plants? You made them angry?"

"You've seen them?" He shakes his head slowly, as he says, "It's just a side effect of creating them. They always disintegrate, eventually. I scoop up the pieces and put them somewhere safe. I loved them all, Pea."

I feel so tired of him, and the way he talks to me. And my feet really hurt.

"So what does the Armillaria want in exchange for this amazing deal? This chance to start yet another jolly big adventure?"

"They only want to conclude the deal they made with the Rampion. They want the Collection."

My Collection.

My father's life goal, and the compressed soul of his first child. Thirty years of my own life and the seeds of a beautiful future. Every Earth flower, given up. Rose and orchid and geranium and begonia and edelweiss and dahlia and dandelion. Lilium longiflorum.

"No."

Hort holds my gaze. I refuse to blink. I do not need to blink.

"It's just a collection," he says, eventually.

"Then why does the Armillaria want it so badly?"

"I don't know!" He laughs. "I don't know everything. Does it matter?"

"Not to you."

"Pea, this is what I've been searching for! A way out of killing everything I touch. That's a good thing, isn't it? You have to admit that's a good thing."

"I thought you were looking for a way to save the universe."

"Same thing!"

"No, it's not. It's not the same thing."

How handsome he is, as he huffs out his frustration at me and smoothes back his hair. "What exactly is the difference?"

I don't want to make this about my own petty concerns, but my petty concern is my home, my family, and my entire planet. "What about Earth? We're not talking about saving Earth any more, are we? You won't infect any new planets, but you don't cure any old ones, right? I'm correct, aren't I?"

"Oh dear," he says.

"What?"

"I was sort of hoping you'd get over that." He grabs my hand, and pulls me through to—

The wheatfield, at night, where the sheaves pop and make the patterns of the stars. We are standing together in the moonlight, although there is no moon. It's so like Earth my heart hurts.

"Look," he says, before I can react. "Look up. Find your home planet. You can't, can you? It's so small. So vanishingly small."

There are white dots and green dots, so many of them. I know Earth is one of the green dots stricken by the virus. But which one? There's no way to tell. This is a task of ordering that's beyond me.

"Now," says Hort. "Try seeing everything this way."

He waves his hand, an insoucient gesture that reminds me of a well-practised magician, and the night sky peels open to form one long horizontal strip. It resembles a roll of paper, each star an impression, rather like complex music for a pianola, if only one could find a device big enough and clever enough to play it.

It starts to scroll, left to right.

New stars, new notes, appear at incredible speed as old ones drop from view. They make no noise. There's only the wind, moving the stalks of the wheat: an eerie noise to accompany the death of thousands of planets, and the birth of thousands more.

"It goes on and on," says Hort. "Death and birth. Did you know birth outweighs death, every time? Our universe expands. It multiplies. It does not end. It's never needed saving. Do you see?"

I'm so dizzy. I sink to my knees. The constant movement

of the sky is making me sick. The ground is, at least, pretending to be solid. I grasp the wheat in my hands. If only it would all stop spinning. Stop growing. How can I ever hope to hold it still, hold it steady?

"And so you see I'm not even really a planet killer, not long-term. I hate destroying all the plant life in the here and now, yes, but once it's all gone life begins again, Pea, it really does. Even on Earth. Do you know how many mass extinctions every planet has, at one point or another? I'd bet your beautiful Earth has had a few. Wiped clean, but it's only a reset, do you get it yet? Hang around, and all new stuff will pop up. That's what happens. That's what always happens. If we returned to Earth now, you'd see it's already happened."

The sky freezes. Then it zips itself back up. I can't tell if I'm doing it or if Hort's doing it. I stand up. I face him. "What do you mean? Are you saying that's already happened? How long has passed?"

"You should probably stay calm," he says. His floppy, stylish hair falls forward to cover one eye and it is lost on me, all his appeal is lost to me. I don't think it will ever come back.

"I am calm. You said the Ingenious Storage Solution was free from time."

"It is! No time passes while you're in here. But there are places out there where it does, and we visited one of them. Castlewellan, remember? Where gravity is so strong, it's inescapable."

"How long?"

He swallows. A long second passes. "Okay, look. It took about half a million years to have a conversation with the Rampion. In my defence, I really thought you'd get over the idea of saving one particular planet. Some of the previous companions did, you see. Some shrugged it off and had a fine time until they degraded."

Lily.

Lily has been dead for over half a million years.

"Take me back. Take me back in time."

"Now that, Pea, I cannot do. This is a chaotic existence at best, but if you were going to give it a classification system according to inevitability you'd put time at the top. It's the eventual master of us all."

Lily.

She's lost to me. She can't come back. I can't save her, see her, touch her, help her, hold her any more, and everything I loved about her is dust, no, not even dust, not even dust.

"It might help if I try to explain it from my perspective," says Hort, and leans forward, reaching out his hands on my head, to put his story in me, but suddenly – for the first and only time since this adventure started – time is on my side. I'm quicker than him. I put my fingers to his temples instead and I force myself within. I rip him open, not caring what I'm losing. I place my tale inside him, and he will carry it for me, and it will eat him. That's what I want. I want him devoured by what he's done.

The Cautionary Tale of Penelope Greensmith
OR – Lost and Found Again

Once upon a time there was an unremarkable and
unimportant planet.

It sustained life. Thriving, balanced and beautiful
beings grew upon it: plants, animals, fungi, bacteria and
viruses could be found, diverse, manifold, and delicate.
One of these beings was called Penelope Greensmith.

Penelope Greensmith was not well travelled,
universally speaking. She had not even really been
very far from England, except on the occasional
holiday. That may be why she held the opinion that
life on Earth was miraculous. She had no idea that
it cropped up everywhere. So perhaps she was
misguided when she decided to continue her father's
work and collect one particular form of life, thinking
she was safeguarding it for the future. She felt
certain a threat was coming to her beloved flowers.

When the threat came, it looked like a good friend.
It wore a pleasant, even handsome, face. It flattered
her, and told her that she was more important than
she had ever thought possible. It persuaded her
to entrust it with her precious flower collection, in
return for the chance to be a hero.

And, in that one transaction, she lost herself.

She lost her planet, too, and her family. These
things were not important, nor remarkable. But
they were all she had.

Penelope Greensmith lost everything she ever loved,
apart from one thing. Her Collection. It still existed. It

offered her hope. It reminded her of everything that was precious about her commonplace world.

But the threat – in reality a selfish, spoiled, unaware and unrepentant idiot who had lost whatever he was when he started out a long time ago, and therefore could be classified as Very Dangerous Indeed – wanted to give away the Collection for his own ends.

At that moment, Penelope found herself once more.

She was a middle-aged woman from a hitherto sheltered existence, and she was very, very angry.

She was angry at all the ongoing, pointless battles she had witnessed: on Earth, in space, as a mother, as a wife, as a person. Angry at all the losses that shaped every creature into what it was. Anger at those who chose to believe that some losses are more or less important than others because of the nature of the creature who experienced them. Anger that there was no way to perceive reality, no system of consciousness that could encompass the scale of all these losses.

Anger that she had to fight for the only thing she had left.

But fight she would.

I have to defend what I believe in, thought Penelope Greensmith, *even if what I am is not an I. Even if I believe is not the absolute truth to anybody else.*

And that was the thought that unified her into a real, proper being once more.

Whether or not she was a morally better being, or a more important one, was a question she would leave for another day.

I take my hands from Hort's head.

He staggers back. His eyes are wide, unfocused. "But that's not right," he said. "That's not how it was at all."

"You can't have the collection," I tell him. "Do you understand, now? My flowers. My father. My Lilium longiflorum." I burn, just like I used to in the middle of the night, when sleep could not come to me.

"But we can start again," he says. "I want us to be together. I'm not good at being alone, you see. I can't be alone. And you're showing remarkable skills. I can't see how you…" He shakes his head, then hits his temple with the heels of his hand. "I'm not— I'm not— I didn't— That's not how it was…"

"You are wrong to ask for it, and I won't give it up."

With those words, he stands up straight. I see the decision flit across his eyes then he pulls himself sideways, and is gone.

The Collection.

I focus my mind on the Storage Room, and pull myself through; by the time I get there, I'm too late. There's only the heel of his green shoe, disappearing. I search for the cardboard box. It's not there. It doesn't come when I call to it.

Think.

Think. There's no time. Think.

There's one thing that might work. One object. I find it, and put it in my cardigan pocket. Then I order my own thoughts, coldly, quickly. Travelling far. Travelling fast. I have to do this, and I have the Rampion's strength and memories to help me. Here's hoping his strong roots keep me together for just long enough to get this done.

I draw a doorway, and set out for Armillaria.

TROUBLE **SWALLOWING**

Penelope Greensmith was home again.

She was standing in her own basement, with familiar things about her. The Vice squatted on the sturdy oak table, and the discs were arranged neatly in their racks, in perfect order. The single light bulb overhead gave the room a warm orange glow, and created shadowed corners.

A single flower rested beside the Vice. Lilium longiflorum. And there was the welcoming aroma of toast, lingering, as if she had made breakfast only a few minutes earlier and then decided to bring it downstairs to get on with her work for the day.

Everything was normal, just for a breath, a moment, and then the room began to curve. The floor bowed away from Penelope whilst the ceiling stretched, and the racks against the walls arced, until the roughly rectangular room was a perfect circle, and Penelope was at its centre, floating, touching nothing at all.

She spun around, looking for the steps that led up to the rest of her cottage. The room turned with her, then continued to rotate even after she stood still. The ongoing movement was not only horizontal; the ceiling moved downwards, and the oak table, with the Vice still upon it, was directly overhead. And where were the stairs? That part of the room simply did not exist. There was instead a fuzzy greyness, a dead spot in her vision. There was no egress from this bubble.

Where was Hort? Where was the Armillaria? Had she used the wrong words, created a doorway to some inescapable place? She breathed, in and out, in and out, fighting against rising panic. Concentrate.

Clarity:

lucidity openness accuracy articulacy limpidity perspicuity purity simplicity transparency

Transparency, yes – the membranous skin of the bubble faded until she could see through the wine racks, the floor, the table and the Vice to the world beyond.

It was—

It was a jungle, verdant, dense, below her, with vast straight Wimba trees reaching up past her bubble to a sky of intense, brilliant blue above.

No. It was an arid, mountainous region with buttes rising high from the flat, dusty land. Saguaro cacti abounded, clumped together in prickly, twisted compositions, while a range of hardy, tough grasses clung to the stern, set faces of the rocks.

Then it was a steppe, stretching far into the distance, unforested, bleak, the ground white with rusty patches of moss and lichen visible here and there, fighting to survive amid the frost.

Maybe this place, between universes, was a little like the Ingenious Storage Solution: neither here nor there, and everywhere in between. A space from which one could travel to other spaces, and of no particular interest in itself.

It was, she thought, rather like an airport.

The steppe turned uniform grey, and a white building erupted from the ground. Overhead, a sunny blue sky appeared. It contained the kind of small, fat clouds that Penelope associated with Britain, sprinting across her field of view, left to right, scudding on the wind.

She turned her attention back to the building. Yes, it had the hallmarks of an airport terminal building, resembling an assemblage of click-together blocks. But it was a small one. She could only spot one runway jutting from it, and that was currently empty. Beside it, there was a glittering square of cars lined up in long-term parking. Strips of grass, trimmed verges, grew between the roads and roundabouts and signposts. Even here, fauna thrived. She saw it, she recognised it. It sprang up between all cracks, asserted its right to live.

A background rumbling: a plane was approaching. She squinted up into the sunshine and spotted it circling, lining itself up for its approach.

It wasn't a plane.

It came closer, banked, straightened. It blinked a vast eye and let out a groan that made the surface of her bubble tremble.

It was a sperm whale.

Such a beautiful creature. Even flying through the sky, it looked magnificent. She had always wanted to see one – had booked a whale-watching trip to Norway a few years ago and then not seen a thing for the entire week and returned home disappointed – and now she was in the presence of one. A whale. The largest brain on the planet. Arteries she could swim through. It was coming towards her. She could see it was not a lonely figure at all, but the centre of its own ecosystem, with so many creatures growing and living upon it.

Seaweed trailed from it in long, streaming strands, and a host of pink flowers erupted from crusty protrusions that were stuck to the folds of its belly. It was an overwhelming experience to be so close; the smell of toast was blotted out by a dense, salty odour with the sweet edge of rot to it. She had read somewhere – she couldn't remember where – about how the smell of a whale was a pungent experience all of its own, as it was home to so many other plants and animals that lived, died and decayed upon it.

Her bubble fell into darkness. The whale was overhead, blotting out the sun, enormous, and coming for her, its mouth opening, opening wider and wider, and the smell, the sight, was beyond anything, bigger than anything, as vast and overpowering as a god.

The whale's mouth was upon her, surrounding her, swallowing her. Engulfed, the sun extinguished, the interior of the mouth was an assault of smell, a riot of cacophonous sounds, a body working with the thumping heart and the sucking breaths deafening. She screamed; was she screaming? She could not hear herself, but she was certain she was making sounds of fear, sounds of panic.

A light.

Just a pinprick of it, through the blanket of black. It was ahead of her, getting larger, larger. The bubble had to be hurtling towards it at an astonishing rate. The light became strong enough to illuminate slick, slippery walls around her. She was in a tube. Then, without warning, the light exploded, and surrounded her.

The bubble slowed to a leisurely pace as it fell into a circular orbit, with many other bubbles around the steady, glowing nub of light which protruded from the floor of the spacious cavern she found herself within. The uneven walls pulsated and glistened. It reminded her of an old film about a craft that was miniaturised and injected into the body of a man. A famous actor – what was his name? – had been devoured by a corpuscle. She fervently hoped there weren't any corpuscles here, but no, all she could see were the other bubbles, which were opaque.

Not all of them – just ahead of her, lower down, circling at the same speed around the growth from the floor, was another transparent sphere, and inside was a figure with floppy brown hair and his shirt sleeves rolled up.

She had to reach him.

Hel

So loud. The voice inside her, blotting out everything, all thoughts and feelings, too enormous and incredible to be comprehensible.

"What?" she screamed.

u?

A consciousness, a giant sentience, asking her something, making an offer on so many levels of possibility, of understanding. She could have asked it anything and it would have opened a negotiation that she did not have a hope of comprehending.

How could anybody possibly trade here, and be certain they had made the right deal? What could such a mind ever want from a creature like her?

She had to try.

"I need to talk to that man in the bubble over there," she said, and was immediately engulfed in a vast wave of incomprehension, emanating from all around her, sinking into her brain.

Wha

"He stole something from me. He doesn't have the authority to trade it with you. To you. For passage to another universe."

It was pointless.

She had translated the whole situation into a particular setup in order to make sense to her, and that meant she was unintelligible to the very thing with which she was now desperate to communicate.

"I have to work within my means," she said to herself, and then, "Car."

Car:

coupe hatchback vehicle motor runabout banger jalopy speedster conveyance wheels wreck freedom limo transport tourer

The bubble shifted, subtly at first, but Penelope kept at it, and pretty soon she was floating in her basement that was the shape of a Volkswagen Beetle.

Her first car had been a Beetle; she had passed her driving test in it, second time, but the initial failure had been due to nerves. She had gone everywhere in that car while at university. She knew it. She reached out her hands, grasping at thin air, and pretended she was holding the steering wheel; she pushed down with her foot, and felt the imaginary accelerator depress.

"Vroom," she said, then indicated with the not-there indicator and pulled out of the orbital ring road to whizz past the bubbles in front of her until she could draw up alongside Hort.

His face, in profile, was calm; was that a slight smile on his lips? He was holding a small, square cardboard box, just like the ones in which he kept his previous companions: the Collection. His eyes were closed. He could not have been aware of her presence. No doubt he thought she could never have reached him, on this planet, let alone in his bubble.

How could she break his concentration?

She did the only thing she could think of. She slowed, created a little distance between them, and then rammed her foot down on the imaginary accelerator, aiming straight for him.

The impact flung Penelope forwards and she hit the front of her bubble with tremendous force at the exact spot where it met with Hort's bubble. Her body prickled with a strange, sucking sensation, and the resistance of the bubble's surface vanished. She pitched forwards, tripped over her own feet and ended up face down on the springy floor of Hort's bubble, which made for a soft cushion. Unhurt, she picked herself up.

The two bubbles had melded together, rather like the way two soap bubbles in the bath might join and become one.

Hort's bubble was so plain. Just an empty space, like the ISS without her flowers or thoughts to give it form. She had, she realised, assumed the ISS's appearance mirrored Hort's inner life, but perhaps that was not it at all. Did Hort not have the facility to picture things in his own way? Where was his own imagination?

Maybe that was why he always needed a companion.

His back was to her; he was unmoved. She walked around him so she could see his face, his expression serene, his eyes still closed: the collision had not stirred him.

"Ahem," she said.

It did no good.

She shook his shoulder very gently, and he opened his eyes slowly, trustingly, like a baby waking from a nap, with a lazy, untroubled blink and a sigh.

"Hello," she said. "You can't trade my Collection."

A smile spread across his face. It could not have been faked; he was genuinely pleased to see her. And she found she was, despite everything, moved by it. "Pea!"

"Actually, it's Penelope."

He blinked a few more times, then stretched. "You've changed again."

"What?" She touched her face, looked down at her body. It was true. She was middle-aged once more. Her stomach and breasts were capacious, and she could feel the sags and wrinkles that had been made through years of laughing, crying, having emotions.

"I prefer it," she said. "Have you done the deal?"

"Yes, it's all done. The Armillaria is opening a gateway now." She followed the line of his pointing finger to look through the transparent skin of the bubble, which was moving away from the light, out of orbit towards a developing patch of reddish, ominous cloud.

"But I told you. You can't trade it."

"How did you even manage to get in here?"

"I smashed the bubbles together."

He rolled his eyes at her. "Amazing. The amount of yourself you must have lost to open a doorway, and you're still not even attempting to get over this being human thing."

"I've decided against it."

"You don't want me in this universe, anyway, do you? I kill every plant I'm near. I'm beginning to think that's an insurmountable obstacle in our relationship."

"It is." She was struggling to find the right words to tell him what she thought of him. She suspected that she had once possessed the words and emotions for this conversation, but they were gone now, which severely limited her options.

"Then let me go, Pea. It'll solve everyone's problems."

"I want my Collection back. Will it...?" She was nervous at the prospect of even mentioning the Armillaria in case it tried to speak to her again in that deafening whale voice. "Would it let you go anyway? Without the flowers to trade?"

He looked steadily at her. There was such a pitying affection for her in his eyes. "That's really not how this works." His gaze flicked past her to the cloud which was growing ever bigger, closer, deepening from red to purple. "If you're not coming with me, I'd suggest you get back in your own—" His mouth moved with no sound forthcoming; then, a moment later, she heard the word, "bubble."

"I can't let you go," she told him, wishing she didn't have to sound like a schoolteacher with an unruly pupil. Couldn't she make him angry, somehow? Or genuinely sorry? Or any emotion that could stir her, both of them, into a different course of action? "I'll have to stop you. I can stop you, you know."

"I don't think you can, but I'm really admiring the effort. Getting out here alone is a major feat, Pea! That deserves a big well done, to start. But I don't suppose you want my approval any more. No, it always ends with them no longer wanting my approval."

He was raising his voice to her, but it was because of a high-pitched whining that had started up, emanating from the cloud, sounding like an old television set warming up.

"Enough," she said. "Give me the box, now, please."

His hands tightened around it. "No, Pea, I'm not going to do that. This is goodbye."

"Please."

"Go home."

abode locale address crib den house flat country continent planet pad quarters roost domicile lodging location safe space place dwelling box caboose

The meanings flew from his mouth and aimed straight for her: sharp, accurate, intended to sting, upset her, break her control apart. Penelope flung up her hands and knocked them aside. "Don't you dare. Don't you even dare."

"I'm just demonstrating that you're not up to taking me on. You're a disintegrating imprint made from two snapshots I made of the personality you used to be. Until you accept you're not even here at all, you'll never be able to make proper sense of the universe."

"I agree," she said. "Luckily, I'm not alone." She steeled herself, put her hands to her chest, and pulled her breasts apart.

Her cottage was inside, but it was no longer a neat space filled with her possessions. A horse chestnut tree in glorious bloom with tall candles of white flowers was rooted in the place where the range cooker had stood, and its branches had spread throughout the rooms. Penelope did not feel its presence as an intrusion in the least; the tree's great roots were holding up the walls of her house. Without it, she would have already stopped existing.

Hort's face was – had she lost an understanding of the expression? She couldn't read him. His eyes were fixed on her chest. The whining was getting louder still, and the colours were deepening again, swirling together into a muddy brown. They were almost inside the cloud.

She had never seen a plant move so fast, but this was the Rampion. Their shared memories told her that it could grow at speed; even so, the branches were springing out of her and across the bubble at a profoundly shocking rate. Hort raised a hand, started to draw a rectangle. The branches surrounded him, pinning his arms to his sides, the pointed leaves growing around him, cloaking him. As the foliage thickened, Penelope found herself being dragged forwards until she was close enough to touch him.

"How?" he asked her.

"I don't know."

"It's not dying. In my presence. It's a real plant, touching me. Holding me." There was such wonder in his expression. Even in a terrible moment of conflict, he could find something to enjoy.

"Pea," he whispered.

She stroked his cheek. He was so young, to her. But to the Rampion, he was different again. He was an old and terrible death for so many creatures. He was unforgiveable.

Reaching into her cardigan pocket, she took out the roll of orange string she had retrieved from the Vice and looped it around the back of his neck. Then she threw the end of the tape over his shoulder to make a complete loop. It was rather like putting a scarf upon him, adjusting it before sending him out into the cold.

"Take him through the Vice," she said.

The box fell, between them, to the floor.

Hort was gone.

She felt a vicious surge of triumph through her trunk, down to her own feet. It threaten to overrun the few pieces of her that were left. A voice inside her said:

I owed him.

"Please," she said. "Please, there are things I still need to do. I need to be myself, just a little longer."

The leaves began to crumple, and turn brown. They dropped from the branches jutting from her chest, then the branches retreated, curling back, until they fitted within her body once more.

Penelope swung her breasts back together, and her skin joined without leaving a seam. She knelt, picked up the box and cradled it on her lap. Had she ever felt so very tired? Of course – after giving birth to Lily. Being split open by another human being, wondering how something so huge, complete, alive, could have dwelt inside her. It was the same exhaustion.

The whining stopped. The swirling brown cloud dissipated.

Whe

red

idh

"He went," she said, once she thought she could divine the Armillaria's meaning. "He had to go. The deal's off."

ego

She could not find her own strength to reply. Instead she relied on the Rampion's roots, knowing she was losing herself utterly in the bargain. But it had to be said.

"NO DEAL."

The crushing disappointment took her breath away. It was such a weight to bear.

But

"They're mine. My flowers. Why do you want them, anyway? They can't mean anything to you. They're so small. So small." She collected herself, and pushed it all into one word:

"WHY?"

It understood her. She could feel its comprehension.

And then it cupped her.

Once, as a child, she had found a baby bird fallen from a nest, trembling, ugly, so exposed and unaware, and she had picked it up and put it back, not knowing what else to do. Should she really try to help it at all? But how could she leave it? This was the same, in so many ways, except she was the bird. She was being held by the vast consciousness of the Armillaria, and it wanted to do right by her. It had goodwill, a desire to explain, and absolutely no idea of how much this communication was costing:

Onc

eup

ona

tim

eth

ere

was

"Stop," she screamed, "Stop. STOP."

The Rampion's consciousness was clear on the matter. The Armillaria was not really a whale, and she was not really inside it. There were no bubbles, and no light. It could take over, and complete the transaction. It offered. It saw the act of assuming control as doing her a favour.

I'll do it my own way, she thought, and the Rampion withdrew its offer. It did not have her completely yet.

How could she trade directly?

An answer came to her: floriography. Speaking through the giving and arranging of flowers. It was often labelled as a Victorian practice, but many cultures had practised it throughout human history. Penelope had developed an interest in it when naming her daughter and had read a thick, calming book about the subject, which had been a welcome distraction through the difficult last days of the pregnancy. A lily, for instance, represented faith. It was an idea that had always appealed to her.

Such an idea could only come from her. She recognised it as her own knowledge: a solution with Penelope Greensmith written all over it.

"Here," she said. "You can't have the Collection. But you can have this."

She reached into the box and pulled out a disc at random, pressing the button to find out what she giving away. It was a bright bloom, a perennial with a long leaf stem, easy to shake in the breeze, shedding its petals easily. An anemone: a fortuitous choice. Named after the Anemoi, the Greek gods of the wind, the anemone represented, in the language of flowers, fragility and loss. Being left behind. Being forsaken. But they could also represent that faint thread of hope that many find in beauty. Such hope can keep a flower rooted, and returning.

She put the disc down on the floor of the bubble, and stepped back. "For you," she said. Then, bracing herself,

"FOR YOU."

There was no reply.

Of course - the Armillaria worked in deals. A trade. What did she want in return?

There were a number of options. The meaning of life, as the Rampion had requested. She felt a surge of longing for that answer, but also a quiet understanding that the need for such knowledge had passed. What, then? Passage to a brand new universe that might make more sense than this one, as Hort had been chasing? An answer to where the Armillaria came from and why it had organised the collecting of flowers in the first place? Or perhaps a look at the Sequoia who apparently ruled her own universe, in some way that Hort had never even got close to specifying? Or a reason why merging with the Rampion created a plant that Hort could not destroy?

Could she ever hope to understand the answers she was given, and if she did, would she still be herself?

Now was not the time for such decisions. She felt the agreement of her passenger. This was a course of action of which it approved.

"You can owe me. # OWE."

The disc clattered, spun, and then erupted into life: anemones, spreading, covering the bubble, so many of them, so beautiful.

Could that be why the Armillaria wanted the flowers? For the exquisite delight that can be had through treasuring the tiniest, most delicate things in this life? It occurred to Penelope that when the largest things made no sense, relief could reside in the smallest objects, the ones that needed so badly to be cherished, instead.

The anemones continued to multiply, covering everything; she could no longer see the chamber outside the bubble. It was time to go. Penelope thought of storage solutions, and, with a shaking hand and practically nothing left to give, managed to draw a doorway.

THE ART OF TRANSLATION

What exactly has happened?

I've been wandering around in the ISS, asking myself that very question.

It's just one more question that won't get an answer.

At first, I found myself in the Storage Room, with its ever-changing shelves. I put the cardboard box that contains my Collection on the highest shelf. It seemed a good place to leave it.

Then I kept pulling myself from room to room, no longer caring about what I was losing. I walked on and on. The Map Room held my attention for a while. I watched the grains of wheat, living and dying in the sky. I perfected the trick of making them roll onwards, like a scroll in a pianola. It's to do with time, that resoundingly difficult concept wrapped up in one handy four-letter word.

Time is not here, of course. Perhaps that's why the Rampion is dormant once more within me.

The Archive was too painful to visit. I didn't want to see that museum in Turin again, not when I couldn't be there in reality, and I was not particularly keen on the idea of watching Hort's adventures in cinematic representation. So instead I worked on creating a new room, all of my own. I drew a doorway and pushed its lines up and down and back and out using the word *extension*, which gave it an interesting quality. The pointed glass roof that bore a line of spikes reminded me of a conservatory that a couple I knew once had built on their first home. We – Graham and I – used to see a lot of them when we were newly married, but after the divorce I never saw them again. I wonder if Graham did. I wonder if he remembered that horrible conservatory until he died. Well, now I have a permanent reminder of my own. It's so strange, how some things stick in your subconscious.

Of all the things I've lost, I really wouldn't have minded losing that.

A blank new room. I could put my own adventures in there. I could perfect turning Tearthumb and Calendula into films in which I'm the hero. But I wonder if that wouldn't make me crave the creation of other adventures. I suspect being the hero is addictive, and I can see a situation where I end up finding an unsuspecting underling on some poor planet, and dragging them along just to witness how brilliant we are – the Rampion/Penelope hybrid – as we all travel across space together.

It would be an easy solution to the eternal problem: that of being alone.

I don't want to do that either, though.

No. I know what I have to do, and with the Conservatory completed, I find the strength to do it.

That's not exactly true. The truth is: I find I've run out of stalling techniques.

So here I stand, back in the main room with the glass steeple and the endless grey outside. I start by summoning lilies. Not just Lilium longiflorum, but many varieties, from the martagon to the canadense, the superbum to the pardalinum. Lilies from all over the world, jostling each other, filling me up with their intense, intoxicating scent.

Then I think of Hort.

I summon him, from the disc that now contains him. He's not difficult to track down. He lies between the Horned Violets and the Hostas.

A small patch of fur appears on the floor, then becomes that floppy brown hair I adore. The surrounding lilies are pushed back as a forehead emerges, then eyes, nose, mouth. Neck, and then the shirt and the trousers, right down to the lace-up shoes, except they are no longer green. They're white.

Hort stands there.

Has he left me a message? Just as Dandelion did for my father? I can't think it would be a love letter, though. Condemnation, maybe, or annoyance. Could he ever be more severe than that? It's surely not in his nature, but I'm afraid of the possibility of it, nonetheless.

But no – no prepared speech kicks in. He does not look like a recording. He looks just like himself.

"Greetings," he says.

He's smiling. He's pleased to see me.

"Can you hear me?" I ask.

"Of course! How are you, Pea?"

"Penelope," I correct him, and he looks so crestfallen that I relent, and say, "Yes, Pea," and then hate myself, a little bit.

"Yes. Pea," he repeats. I can see it doesn't connect with him, not really. "Am I quite myself, do you know?"

"You look like you. You sound like you."

"You think so? Look at these, though!" He frowns at his shoes, then says, "Do you know, there are still such exciting things to see out there. We should get out there again! The universe is waiting for us! I'll show you around some of the most amazing sights. Formal gardens you wouldn't believe. I'm so glad we share a specialist interest. There's so much for us to talk about, isn't there?" He rattles on, filled with enthusiasm, describing plants and places and people and perfect experiences. He is charming and effervescent. He's the Hort I've always liked best. "There's nothing like the thrill of arrival in a totally new place, is there? It makes you forget yourself. Let's go right now, shall we? Here, take my hand."

I reach out, and we hold hands. I can feel his warm, strong grip. Hort's hand. How can that be? But it is. It is.

"We're off," he says.

He doesn't move. Doesn't attempt to draw a doorway. "Is it just me, or is everything very flat?"

"Flat? How so?"

"I don't know, exactly. Flat. Where there used to be layers. And gaps between layers."

"You got compressed," I tell him. "In the Vice."

"Well. That must be it, then." We're still holding hands. "Yes. That must be it."

"I'm leaving," I tell him. "I'm afraid you have to stay here. But it'll be fine."

"Will I be alone? I'm not too good at alone."

A solution comes to me. "No. You won't be alone. I promise."

"Okay then. Will you come back?"

So, at the very end, he's managed to trap me into telling him a lie. It comes easily to me. "Yes, of course. I'll be right back."

He nods. Then holds out his arms, and I hug him. I hug him with all the love and hate I feel for him. He's unique.

> • ‹

Afterwards, I retrieve my Collection from the Storage Room and take it to the soft, sleeping Cynarans, curled up tight. They gather around me as I reach into the cardboard box and take out Hort's disc.

I stretch out my hand and they cluster to him. They surround him, and absorb him into themselves. I have no idea what they think of him in this new form, but I like to imagine they're pleased to see him.

And, at the very least, he won't be alone.

LILY, TO SEED

Lily: Maybe some day, in the future,
somebody will have survived this
time and will find this phone
and will see these messages and
- I don't know what difference
that will make. None, to me.
None at all.

[Pause.]

Lily: Dad died this morning. The
swamp dried to a black powder,
and we'd run out of food, and
he insisted on eating some to
see if it could sustain us. But
it's poison. I would eat some
myself, but it was not a good
way to... I can't do that to
myself. I'm all I have left.
Besides, I don't think it
will matter much. This black

dust is everywhere now. The
wind keeps stirring it up and
it's getting darker and darker.
Soon it will blot out the sun
entirely and that will certainly
kill everything that isn't
already dead. It's so much
colder. I wonder how low the
temperature will get.

[Pause.]

Lily: It means the solar charger is
useless, too.

[Pause.]

Lily: Look at me. Worrying about
how I'm going to charge my
phone, to the last. I suppose
some thoughts are programmed
down deep, after a while.
Inescapable. While other things
are so hard to come by. Like
trust. Like love. Like faith. I
hope there is a life after death
in some form, but if only
there was a scrap of proof. I'd
feel so much better. Kieran?
Dad? Mum, are you there? If
you're there, give me a sign.

Anything. Please.

[Pause.]

Lily: It would be ironic if the first
        actual recorded evidence of the
        afterlife was taken shortly
        before the end of the world.

[Pause.]

Lily: The battery is nearly out.
        See you soon, everyone. I love
        you, no matter what I ever
        said to the contrary. If I
        raged, if I shouted, if I chose
        not to speak at all, it was only
        because I didn't understand.
        I thought the reason I was here
        was to understand the
        experience. Now, I'm not so
        sure. I think maybe Dad was
        right, all along. There's only
        kindness. Deep down, that's the
        one thing that's left.

PLANTED

For the longest time I thought the world would end.

I realise now that what I meant was something very different. I thought I would end. That things familiar to me would end before I did, and it would be a terrible experience.

I didn't really know what terrible was.

That's fine, I find, in retrospect. For now I don't know what anything means, and there is no terrible and no wonderful that I can grasp in an objective manner. Everything is only experienced in my own unique, miniscule way. Which brings me to the greatest and most inconsequential epithet of all time:

Living is pointless, and it is all I've got.

The Rampion stirs within me. Right now he's mute and comforting, which is helpful because this Earth is a confusing place. It's not barren. I thought I would be bringing my Collection back to a dead world, but the rich, loamy soil is fertile, and plants have sprung up. I'm standing in a field of tall, healthy leucospermums, evergreen shrubs; how could they have survived?

I try speaking to them. "Can you hear me?" This would seem to be my opening gambit when dealing with the unknown. *Can you hear me?* Ridiculous.

They don't reply.

As I had constructed the doorway to take me back to Earth, I thought of home. My cottage. Is this the very spot where my cottage stood? Is this the ground where my daughter died? There's no way to ever know – another unanswerable question – but I find myself looking for a sign anyway. It would have been half a million years ago, or more.

A sign, please. A lily. Let there be a lily here.

No. There's nothing. What could possibly survive for such a length of time? Apart from, obviously, leucospermums.

I think I read an article once, about the successful growing of very old seeds, that had been stored for hundreds of years. Wasn't that a leucospermum? Maybe some seeds buried down deep, so deep that they survived Hort's virus, and waited for their time to come around again. Seeds are so hardy. The tiniest of objects, and they can lie dormant until the right moment. They can even travel through space and still decide when to wake up, and when to grow.

Now.

The Rampion is fully awake inside me. I feel its roots twist.

"This is a good planet for growing," I tell him. "But there's a condition. You need to let the other plants grow too. Leave them room, and sun and nutrients. They're very dear to me."

I feel his reluctance to agree to such a condition. He's the Rampion. He should be dominant.

"I took you in. I gave you a place to wait. You owe me."

Yes. I owe you. We owe each other.

But I feel his acquiescence to my terms, and he might be lying, but there's nothing I can do about that now. I put down the Collection, and pull apart my breasts, splitting myself open. The Rampion is a thick mass of twisted trunk and branch; I'm simply the husk around him.

"The Collection," I say.

You. It's yours to wake.

"How?"

Tell it.

And so I say, "Open."

Open:

expel aerate purify vent oxygenate fan expose truthful honest straight square forthright frank uncover unfold unimpede clear free wide empty expand expose peel rent roll strip obvious amenable allow

The cardboard box disintegrates to dust. The words exist. They have form; they swoop and hang in the sky. They keep pouring from me, and they each pick up a disc and carry them away, gaining distance, height: they will scatter the seeds. They will repopulate this earth:

Dahlia, Zinnia, Alyssa, Acacia, Magnolia, Peony, Rose, Ivy, Sunflower, Violet, Gardenia, Daffodil, Gerbera, Baby's Breath, Solidaster, Snapdragon

There are so many more, but I cannot think of their names, their names are leaving me, and there was a flower I loved, a tall, graceful flower, but that name has gone too, as has my own. There is a tree inside me. Its trunk is in my mouth. It forces its branches out through my arms, my head, and its roots emerge through my old, tired feet to spike me to the ground.

But all it takes is a shift of thought: I'm not the husk at all. Not the remains, but the tree itself. I'm in the uppermost branches, and down in the soil. I will grow long and strong here. We will. We will grow together.

Will we survive? What would it mean, to survive?
Does it matter?
All that matters
after all
after everything
is that
the journey
was
interesting.

AFTERWORD

The Peter Cook quote at the beginning of the book comes from an interview he did with Alan Titchmarsh in 1994, back when *Pebble Mill* (a light entertainment and chat show) used to be shown on BBC1 most lunchtimes. I remember listening to him rebut the idea of potential, and of achieving what others think should be achieved. It has stayed with me since. I only recently found out that it was his last television interview, and that it is lost, as are most of the recordings of *Pebble Mill*, so I can't check exactly what he said. This version of the quote comes only from my memory. I hope I got it right.

The quote on page 125 belongs to a different Peter: Peter Ustinov.

There have been a number of versions of the quote Penelope remembers when she first comes across Hort's Collection; the one used on page 84 is from *The Electronic Library* by J.E. Rowley, originally published in 1998.

THE LOOSENING SKIN

SKIN

ALIYA WHITELEY

☆ **2019 ARTHUR C. CLARKE AWARD FINALIST**
☆ **2019 JOHN W. CAMPBELL AWARDS FINALIST**
☆ **2019 BRITISH FANTASY AWARDS FNIALIST**
☆ **2019 BRAVE NEW WORDS AWARD LONGLIST**

Rose Allington is a bodyguard who suffers from a rare disease. Her moults come quickly, changing everything about her life – who she loves, who she trusts.

In a world where people shed their skin, it's a fact of life that we cast off our old lives. But those memories of love can be touched – and bought – if you know the right people.

Rose's former client, superstar actor Max Black, is hooked on Suscutin, a new wonderdrug that prevents the moult. Max knows his skins are priceless, and moulting could cost him his career.

When one of his skins is stolen, and the theft is an inside job, Max needs the best who ever worked for him - even if she's not the same person.

ALWAYS NORTH

VICKI JARRETT

"Compelling, beautifully estranging and wonderfully urgent in its imaginative passion."
Adam Roberts, author of *The Thing Itself* and many more

☆ 2019 KITSCHIES AWARD FINALIST
☆ THE GUARDIAN'S AND FINANCIAL TIMES' BEST SCIENCE FICTION OF 2019

We all have to work to live, even if it is an illegal survey for oil in the rapidly melting arctic.

Isabel is part of a weathered crew of sailors, scientists and corporate officers she sails into the Arctic. A great icebreaker carves into the brutal environment, and the days grow longer, time ever more detached, as they pass through the endless white expanse of the ice.

But they are not alone. They have attracted the attention of seals, gulls and a hungry, dedicated polar bear. The journey to plunder one of the few remaining resources the planet has to offer must endure the ravages of the ice, the bear and time itself.

This is what we find when we travel – *Always North*.

www.unsungstories.co.uk/alwaysnorth
Follow Vicki 🐦 @Vicki_Jarrett